The Weight of a Feather and other stories

by

Judy Croome

The stories in this anthology are works of fiction. Names, characters, places and incidents are either the product of the author's imagination or are used fictitiously, and any resemblance to actual persons, living or dead, or to actual events or locales is entirely coincidental.

Cover Design: Melissa Williams
http://mwcoverdesign.blogspot.com

Cover Image:
Purchased from http://www.istockphoto.com/

Editor: Angela Voges
Typographica Manuscript http://www.typographica.co.za/

First Print Edition: 3 November 2013
ISBN: 978-0-9870447-3-0

Published by Aztar Press

Dedication

This collection of stories is dedicated to my mother

Naomi Dawn Heinemann

The indelible fingerprints of her love are found in her inspiring example to her daughters and granddaughters; her constant encouragement that has sustained me throughout my life, and in her unwavering kindness to those vulnerable souls and strangers who, needing a helping hand in an often cruel world, find a safe refuge under her wings.

And, as always, for

Beric John Croome

My husband, my lover and my very best friend.

Acknowledgments

Some of the stories in this collection have appeared in the following publications: *The Huffington Post* (Featured Fifty Fiction), *Itch* Magazine, *Notes from Underground*, *The Fall: Tales from the Apocalypse* and *Variations on a Theme*.

Thanks to my writing friends and colleagues, Debs, Leonie and Janet, without whose technical input and morale boosting encouragement these stories would not have been written.

Particular thanks are due to my husband, Beric Croome, and my mother, Dawn Heinemann, for their constant belief in both me and my writing. I must also thank my sister Iona and her husband, Ian Cockerill, my niece Nikki and her husband Gareth Deiner, my niece Bailey Cockerill, and my nephew Michael Cockerill and his friend Sophie le Butt for their interest and support.

I am also grateful to Melissa Williams of MW Cover Design for the beautiful cover design, and to Angela Voges, for her editing skills and insightful comments.

While the creative expression of all stories included in this anthology is mine, the ideas that formed the basis of four stories belong to others. For these brilliant concepts, I must sincerely thank the following people: our dear friend, Justine Limpitlaw (*The Weight of a Feather*); Hennie and Sandra Cronje, the convivial hosts of De Oude Huize in Harrismith (*Jannie Vermaak's New Bicycle*); George Orwell's *Animal Farm* (*Rainbow Farm*); and Anton Chekov's *The Huntsman* (*The Gold Miner*, 1st runner-up in the *Variations on a Theme* competition, later published in an anthology by The Literary Lab). These all sparked the ideas that became the original stories included in this anthology.

Judy Croome (2013)

Contents

The Weight of a Feather

Moyra Kincaid's bantam cock, Apollo, greets the dawn every morning with a cry far bigger than one would expect from such a little bird.

On her eighth birthday, she lies in bed, watching the daybreak seep through the hole in the curtain that her Ma tried to mend once more, listening to the first few caws as he clears his throat. Then his serenade starts; louder than usual today, she smiles, knowing he's wishing her a happy birthday.

On and on he sings, until she hears Pa grumble to Ma, "Shut the bird up, Alice, or I'll do it."

There's a squeak—her parents' bed is as old as her curtains—and a sigh. She scrambles to her knees, watching through the window, as Ma comes out the back door, hair mussed from sleep, her faded pink nightgown flapping around her slippered feet.

"Shoo!" Ma's noise doesn't even cause a hitch in Apollo's voice. He croons even louder, until a slipper nicking his tail feathers ends his performance.

Laughing at his disgruntled squawk, Moyra scrambles back beneath the covers. She'll wait until Ma comes in. Pretending to be asleep, she'll let Ma wake her, bringing her the present. Never big, it's always just something small Ma makes: a doll's dress or a special cake. It's not much, but to Moyra, it means the world.

This year there is no present.

"Your brain will freeze, sleeping so late," Ma says, and pulls open the curtains. Moyra peeps at her over the top of the blanket, straining to see what she's carrying. "It's a school day. Hurry up!" She turns, and Moyra sees her hands are empty. "And you must feed the bantams before you go—we want them fat and juicy, don't we?"

She sees the beginnings of a smile on Ma's face. Relieved, she smiles back. This must be a game. Ma knows it's her birthday, and she wants it to be a surprise. So, Moyra plays along, slipping her skinny legs over the edge of the bed, so they shrivel with the cold of the cement floor as she says, "School finishes early today."

"I know," says Ma, and her smile gets broader. "You'll be home in time for lunch." She runs a hand through the tangled hair on Moyra's head. "You're getting to be such a big girl now," and the child wonders why her mother's smile suddenly looks sadder.

But she forgets that in the excitement of rushing to school; of seeing her class gathered at the school gates, holding hand-painted cards that say "Happy Birthday, Moyra!" There are no presents—none of them are rich. She's heard Ma complain to Pa, that she never wanted to live in a poor neighbourhood, to be so poor it's a battle to put food on the table, but today Moyra lives in the richest neighbourhood in town. The teacher makes a paper crown for her, and the class sings happy birthday, even awful Billy Jones who, every day, steals the jam sandwich Ma packs for her lunch.

Today she's not shy Moyra Kincaid, with freckles and her curious, nosy-parker mind. Today she's one of them.

Closing her eyes in bliss, she thinks of Apollo and Daphne, her best friends. When they hear the rattle of the corn feed against the aluminium bucket, they crowd around her, seeming like twenty not two, in their eagerness to peck the golden kernels off her palm. She laughs in time to their cackling and whispers her secrets to them as they search busily for the last few grains of corn.

"It's Sally-Anne's birthday party on Saturday," she says. "But I'm not invited." She scratches Apollo's head and he gives a comforting chirrup. "It's my freckles."

Or, "I got full marks in the algebra test. Teacher likes me but," she tells Daphne, throwing a handful of seed to the little brown-and-white hen, "the others hissed at me." When the bird only ruffles her feathers before scratching busily at the ground in search of more food, it makes an odd sense to Moyra. We love you, Daphne tells her, it's not so important that *they* like you.

But today, on this special day, she can tell them that, for once, they aren't her only friends. Today the whole world is a friend to Moyra Kincaid.

When the bell rings to free them from school Moyra, still flushed from the excitement of the day, dawdles. She lingers, extracting the last joy from the day, before carefully removing the paper crown and putting it in her satchel so it won't tear before she gets it home to show Apollo and Daphne.

Ma and Pa are waiting for her at the gate and, until she sees their smiles, she wonders why Pa is home from work so early.

"Happy Birthday, Moyra, love," they chorus as she unlatches the gate, and they fuss over her crown and tell her how big she's getting.

"Go and wash up, lunch is nearly ready," Ma says, and smiles the same smile she did when she woke Moyra. "I've cooked a special treat for your birthday."

And Moyra laughs as she remembers her momentary fear of this morning, that Ma had forgotten her birthday. Quickly changing out of her school uniform, she hangs it up neatly as Ma has taught her. Carefully arranging her paper crown on her hair, she hurries into the backyard, pausing only to collect a bucket of corn.

"Apollo! Daphne!" she calls, rattling the corn in the bucket. When they don't come, she clicks her tongue against her palate, her special call for them. "Apollo?" She shakes the corn round and round, the noise loud enough to call them from the farthest corners of their backyard kingdom. "Daphne?"

"They're gone," her Pa says from the back door.

"Where?" she asks.

"In there." He jerks his head back towards the house, sniffing the air like a bloodhound on a scent.

She sniffs, too, not smelling anything except the special lunch Ma has cooked. "Did Ma let them in the house for my birthday?" she asks.

Pa guffaws so loud, he has to take his crisp, white handkerchief out to wipe a bubble of spit from the corner of his mouth. "You could say that," he chortles, "but only as far as the kitchen."

It's then that she sees the pile of bloody newspapers by the dustbin; a few feathers stick out from the haphazard folds. "No-o-o!" she cries, and the aluminium bucket clutters to the ground as she drags her hands upwards to cover her eyes and block the sight out. "I won't eat! I won't eat!" she cries, a litany of pain searing her heart.

"You will," Pa says sternly, "or you'll go hungry, birthday or not!"

"They're my *friends.*"

Pa looks at her strangely. "They're stupid birds," he says. "They can't be your friends."

How can she explain to him what they meant to her? She doesn't even try. She knows Pa won't change his mind. "I won't eat," she whispers. "How can I eat them?"

Clumsily, Pa pats her shoulder. "You'll get over it," he says. "After all, they're just birds." With one last pat, he turns back to the house. "Tidy up here. Lunch will be ready soon."

As he disappears into the kitchen, she hunches down and picks a feather up off the ground. Forlorn white fluff, speckled with brown, she weighs it in her palm. So light, she can hardly feel it. Beyond this, did Apollo and Daphne exist outside her mind? Did she dream their friendship? Or was it as insubstantial as the weight of the feather she holds?

An hour later, when Pa calls her to eat, she lets the feather fall. A breath of wind lifts it, sucking it through the ragged wire fence. It snags for a second, as if saying a final goodbye, but then the wind picks up speed. Absently, Moyra wipes the last of the moisture from her cheeks.

"Coming, Pa," she finally says, as he calls her again.

She goes to wash her hands—removing her paper crown, she crumbles it into a discarded ball—and returns to the kitchen. Sliding into her usual seat at the table, she's mortified when her tummy growls loudly at the warm fragrance seeping from the casserole dish as Ma lifts the lid.

"Are you hungry, love?" Ma asks, smiling. "It's your favourite," her mother adds, "Chicken casserole, especially for your birthday."

Ma heaps her plate high and the saliva gathers under Moyra's tongue. Waiting, as Ma serves the others, she idly picks at a sliver of chicken from her plate, moist with thick brown gravy. Is this Apollo, she thinks? No, she tells herself quickly, it's just a stupid bird.

As she holds out her plate for a second helping, she doesn't yet realise that this birthday is the one she'll remember for all her years to come. For it's the day she puts aside her innocence. Chickens, she learns, are just birds; they aren't for loving. Love is a foolish dream, too dangerous for the heart. Oh yes, she grows up that birthday, for she never again allows herself to love.

Except, perhaps, for the old photograph she buys at a garage sale twenty years later. Old, the glass cracked across the top corner, she pays the price without bargaining. Back at her apartment, she gently dusts it off, and hangs it in her bedroom, where she can see it from her bed.

There's a wooden rail, with a small bantam rooster perched proudly on it, looking down at his brown speckled hen, busily pecking golden corn spilling from an up-ended aluminium bucket. Not everyone's ideal photograph, but Moyra greets it first thing every morning.

"Hello, Apollo," she whispers, then touches a finger to the busy little hen, frozen in eternal motion through the lens of a camera. "Hello, Daphne."

And, for the first time in years, her heart flickers with more than loneliness. She calls it heartburn, blaming the hamburger she ate for lunch. Others, though, would call it love.

The Weight of a Feather *was first published by The Huffington Post (USA) Featured Fiction Fifty series in May 2013.*

One Lonely Road

A dusty strip, the road starts nowhere and stretches into tomorrow. It sits, desiccating the lives of those who dare to travel it.

The farmer, broken by one drought too many, ties the trailer to his tractor, loads it with his possessions—there was space for a few of his scrawny chickens—and chugs down the road, his tears as dried out as the river he leaves behind.

The city visitors race along, until a sharp stone pierces the tyre of their luxury vehicle, ripping a gaping hole into the speeding rubber. The woman's high-pitched voice complains incessantly about the discomfort, but it takes them ten minutes to realise the tyre's in shreds. They skid to a halt, the passenger door opening so that one elegant high-heeled shoe can totter onto the road.

"Oh no, doll," the voice squeals. "We've got a puncture."

And the road chuckles, sending dust and a solitary tumbleweed rippling along its length, staining those glittering shoes with terracotta dust.

But it's the old man's company the road enjoys the most, with his weather-beaten face as corrugated as the road itself. He pads along on leathery feet, so softly the road hardly knows he's there. Stopping occasionally, he lifts a rough hand to shade his eyes and stares down the length of the road. His eyes narrow with the strain; eventually he nods in confirmation and continues doggedly on his way.

The road heaves a sigh of relief. It knows the old man will not leave its winding length. Not until he finds the oasis he's been searching for, all these years of his life.

Born Beneath a Balsamic Moon

The sight of the solitary figure, hunched warmly in tattered animal skins, stops the slow drag of my feet. The flickering flames draw me towards their heat, into the clearing where he sits, unhidden. I hadn't seen him until the hiss of a falling log broke the stark silence surrounding me.

"What do you want?" He speaks rustily, a high-pitched squeak scrubbing the hairs of my neck into attention.

"A drink." I take a step closer, exhaustion pushing me to ignore the creeping darkness. "Some food, if you can spare it."

"What else?"

"A place to rest."

"Why here?"

Patiently I answer his questions. A stranger intruding in his domain, I need him. "There's nowhere else for me to go." I gesture towards the thin sliver of moon, still low in the night sky. "There's not enough light to go on."

"But you don't want to go on, do you?"

An inescapable truth lies embedded in his words. I shake my head. "There's no future for me here."

A foot scrapes along a rock as he bends to pick up a stick. Poking the fire into a greater blaze, he says, "Sit."

So I sit, stumbling over my weary feet in unseemly haste, my stomach grumbling loudly in protest. I'd begun my journey ill prepared; now I'm paying for my foolishness.

He holds out an old tin cup. I gratefully press my palms around the fading image of Spiderman. It reminds me of Marty.

I try not to think of Marty, but it's easier to stop breathing than to stop remembering the last time I saw him.

"You've been thinking of killing yourself. That's why you came here."

Coffee, hot and acrid, slops over my hands. "Suicide is for cowards," I whisper in denial.

"Or desperate souls."

Desperate? Am I desperate? A hollow cavern, musty, rotten and black as the Devil's eyes, exists where other people have hearts.

Perhaps I am desperate, and it shows on my face. I haven't looked in a mirror for days, so I've noticed no changes.

"Is there nothing to live for?"

An eternity of love mellows the intrusive question. I lift my gaze from the flames and, until my eyes adjust, I think my companion is merely an illusion, another part of my madness.

I answer him anyway. "Nothing. No one." Hopelessness thrums through my answer and, so there can be no misunderstanding, I add, "I'm alone in a world gone mad."

"We're alone all our lives." He chuckles, deepening the crevices lining his face with years of living. "And this world has always been mad."

I look around. Despite the dimness of dusk, there is peace and beauty here. This is not the black void of petty sins, nor is it the chaos consuming my soul since Marty left me.

"There's no madness here."

A malignant flicker escapes from his eyes, eating deep into my secret fears. "You're wrong."

I jerk upwards, needing only the tiniest excuse to flee once again. He knows what he's done and smiles, revealing a row of yellowed teeth. "You're in no danger from me," he soothes, and the warmth returns to his words, seeping into my loneliness.

Can I trust him?

I have no choice, and no energy, to do otherwise.

"Where," I clear my throat, the dryness of fear clicking away the last taste of coffee, "is the madness here?"

He's silent, staring into the smouldering embers for a long while. The faint swish as he twirls the coffee dregs in his mug—another dented superhero stares at me through his grubby fingers—is all that breaks the intense silence of the night. Just when I think he won't answer me, he says, "Close," and a shudder racks his slight frame, stirring the mangy fur slung around his shoulders. "Too close."

A jackal yip-yips in the distance and, in unison, we shift nearer the fire. His bony knee knocks against my denim-clad leg, and then he whispers invitingly, "Tell me of your madness."

Does he ask because he wants to distract himself from his own insanity? Or does he want to know what brought me into his solitude?

"There's no reason to go on."

"Reason has so little to do with life." He takes my hand in a surprisingly feminine gesture of comfort, cupping it between his palms and gently rubbing it. "It's in the heart that people find the strength to go on."

"I have no heart any more." I don't even try to hide the bitterness. Or the anger. "I lost it a year ago."

"When Marty left."

The pain is numbing; I don't question how he knows.

"Will you tell me what happened?"

I shake my head. I've told no one. For, if I open my jaws, still locked in agony—if I let one word spill out of me, the pus of despair will choke me.

"Tell me." There's an order in the sudden deepening of the stranger's voice. Still I resist. I've held it in for so many months I don't know how to speak of the emptiness that fills me.

"Tell me ... please."

I loosen my tongue from the sticky flytrap that is my palate to say no. Somehow what I say is not what I intend.

"It happened in the middle of the day," I begin, "a beautiful spring day, full of hope and happiness ..."

#

"Marty," I call, "hurry up! You'll be late again." I hear the careless clatter as he runs down the stairs, followed by the familiar thud of the heavy bag landing in the corner.

"I'm here, Ma," and the whirlwind that is my son slumps into momentary quiet as he slurps his juice, Spiderman's vapid face rapidly fading from orange to crystal clear as the tumbler empties. "Yum," Marty says, "Chocbitz!" and begins to demolish his cereal. Already, he's loosened his tie and his hair, neatly combed before he left the bathroom, is spiked and on end.

The familiar tightness expands my chest. I don't often allow myself regrets, but today I can't help thinking if only his father could see him now. Sighing, I turn back to the dishes piled high in the sink, knowing it's too late for regrets. Jonathon is gone, long gone, the car crash that killed him almost forgotten. Only I am left to cherish the milestones marking our son's journey to maturity.

Too soon, it's time to leave for work. Dull as it is, it's secure and pays the bills that keep my Marty safe. I drop him off at school on the way.

There's nothing extraordinary about the start of this particular day—the morning passes with the usual office ho-hum. I clear two tapes of dictation quickly and even some long-outstanding filing. Soon the moment I wait for every day arrives. I must fetch Marty from school.

I'm slightly late today. A traffic snarl delays me, so I park across the road, half a block away from the school gates. Marty emerges from the pack of noisy children in a rush, his satchel on his back, his hands clutching a large poster.

Even from this distance, I pick up his eagerness, and I smile lovingly. He had his art class today. From experience, I know the poster is a gift for me. Perhaps another heart, roughly drawn and asymmetrical, but full of so much love the mother in me will somehow find an empty spot in our tiny apartment to pin it up.

He looks toward the spot where I normally park and frowns when I'm not there. Since Jonathon died, he hates it when I'm late.

"Marty," I call, standing on tiptoe to wave at him. "I'm over here, Marty."

"Ma!" He shouts delightedly, holding his drawing aloft, "Look what I've got for you!"

With his characteristic excess of energy, he charges towards me, all his focus on reaching me.

Neither of us sees the car until it's too late.

Far, far too late to do anything except watch, in silent, stunned horror, as my son's small body flies up, over the festive red roof, to land crumpled and still at the side of the road.

Blood dribbles slowly towards the words he has written across his paper offering. *I love Mom*, I read.

Calmly, too calmly, I scoop it up, folding it in two, before slipping it into my purse. Only then do I kneel next to my son. "I love you too, Marty," I say. I barely hear the screams around me, fading into the sounds of an approaching siren, or feel the hands gently unclasp my grip from Marty's still warm fingers ...

#

In the distance, I hear someone sobbing, and I know it's me. I haven't cried once since Marty died, and my throat struggles to cope with the deluge pouring from my heart. The stranger lets me cry until I'm empty of all tears; limp and drained dry amidst the rubble of my life.

"It's not fair!" I don't bother to hide the acid quagmire consuming me. "First Jonathon, then Marty. Why take both of them? Why leave me alone?"

"The madness doesn't discriminate."

"I want to see Marty." The sobs rise in my chest once more but, ruthlessly, I crush them. Crying has made no difference. I am still alone. "I need to see my son again. I need to know he's alright before I go crazy. I may as well be dead too!"

"Will only the silence of death make the madness leave you?"

My muscles are locked with the tension of keeping myself from breaking up, but I manage a tremor of assent. He smiles mysteriously. "Look at the fire."

My gaze shifts to the glowing amber coals and the air gets heavier, sweeter. I sway towards the dying fire, close, too close, so some part of me smells the singe of burning hair. I've been cold for so long, I relish the sudden heat on my cheeks.

A breeze springs up, rustling through the leaves and stoking the somnolent coals into new life. A life which flickers and flares into an all too familiar sight. Hardly believing what I see, I stumble to my knees, crying, "Marty!"

And, before he leaves as quickly as he left me a year ago, I reach out to touch him, to hold my beloved son just once more. I want to tell him all I never had the chance to say before: my hopes for his future; my dreams for his life. To say I know the child he'd been would grow into a man, a good and decent man, loving and loved.

Oh-so-loved for, without him, my life is hollow, as thin and faded as the waning crescent moon hanging forlornly above us. The crackling coals merge until I see a face, a child's face, with Marty's eyes and Marty's mouth.

"I love you, Mom," he says. "We'll meet again, but not yet ... not yet ..." and his precious image melts back into mere flames.

I thrust forward, wanting to embrace him close to my heart, so it can beat anew, instead of lying there cracked, my life's blood trickling out with every memory. The pain jolts up my arms, searing a path directly into my chest, but I hardly notice it. "Don't leave me, Marty," I scream, "Oh God, please don't leave me alone!"

I jump up, kicking the coals apart, searching for him, desperate for him to stay.

But my son leaves me, as he did before.

This time I'm left clutching nothing but a smouldering stick. I chant my grief in a crescendo of pain as the blisters on my palms sear their way into the cavern of my chest, incinerating my broken heart into a pile of lifeless charcoal. "Marty," I cry, "Marty! Marty! Mar—"

"Hush, child, hush." The stranger's touch on my cheek is gentle and calming. "Be quiet and listen."

Slowly I contain my grief. In the stillness, I hear the distant beat of a drum, faint and faltering, an erratic rhythm slowly surrendering into the peace of acceptance. It is my heart, I realise, the wound I'd feared mortal now cauterised as my life begins to creep back into being.

Dazed with emotions I'd thought diminished forever in the moment I last held Marty's hand, I look around me, hardly taking in the shadows cast by the faint moonshine.

"I'm alive," I say. Even I hear how surprised I sound. "I'm not dying any more."

"An end is not loss." As he speaks, the stranger nudges more logs on the fire. "It's simply ... an end." He stands up, dusting charcoal from his palms. "Or a beginning. Give me your hands." Obedient to his authority, I place my hands in his and, no longer feeling the aching blisters, my attention is held as he speaks.

"The balsamic moon gathers wisdom into the soul." I must strain forward to hear his whisper. "Look up," he continues, "and see your future."

Ten minutes ago I would have seen nothing but the remnants of a soul shorn of hope, too weary to go forward. When I look at it now, somehow the thin crescent is no longer sad and waning, but holds a glimmer of new life.

In a gasp of gratitude, I seek out the stranger, but he's no longer with me. I am alone again, only the blood pulsing fiercely in my veins keeping me company.

For a moment, the old fears rise to devour me. Then the victory screech of an owl almost drowns out the last, fated squeal of its prey.

The owl will live, gaining strength from the gift it encountered in the inconspicuous moonlight.

And, so too, will I.

Calm again, I put my fears aside as, easing the last tension from my spine, I stretch and yawn widely. Tomorrow, I will visit Marty's grave. Then I will return to my life, desolate no longer, but abundant with memories.

For tonight, though, I will sleep peacefully, perhaps dreaming of Marty again. Perhaps not, for I no longer yearn to see him. He is with me whenever, and wherever, I want—in the battered Spiderman cup lying discarded at my feet and in the shadows cast as the moon moves inexorably onwards into a new day, a new cycle.

It is over, and it is here, beneath a balsamic moon, that I am born again.

Born Beneath a Balsamic Moon *first appeared in ITCH magazine, an online periodical published by the University of the Witwatersrand's School of Literature, Language and Media (South Africa) in November 2010.*

The Biter Bit

Sliding behind the steering wheel of my new silver Audi, I slammed the door shut, ignoring the rattle of the wooden rosary hanging from the rear-view mirror.

"How could you?" I asked.

"In my defence …"

"There *is* no defence!" I clicked my safety belt in with a sharp snap. "Douglas is *blind*! Look at him."

With petulant reluctance, his gaze followed my out-flung arm to rest on the old man hunched on the empty red Coke crate outside the Spar. Douglas, his milky blue eyes staring into a world only he could see and his forehead propped up by the thin white cane, was without his customary broad smile.

"I know," my husband said, more two-year-old toddler than well-respected headmaster.

"Then why did you steal from his collection cup?" In the silence that followed I slammed the steering wheel with the flat of my hand. "*Why?*"

"I forgot to draw cash from the ATM and I wanted to buy a Lotto ticket."

As if that was an excuse.

The woman from the home-bake store next to the Spar was glaring in our direction as she carefully curled Douglas's fingers around a cup of steaming coffee. My husband shifted in the car seat, his hand half reaching towards me. "If I'd won I was going to share the winnings with Douglas."

"Sure," I snorted.

He sunk back down into the hot leather. "I'll make it up to him!"

"That you will," I promised, looking at the woman hovering over Douglas.

"I'm collecting money for an extra room on Douglas's RDP house," she'd said last week, her smile that of a nervous supplicant.

"I'm sorry," I'd said. "My husband doesn't approve of charity. He says he pays his taxes and people should help themselves if the government won't help them."

Today, as our gazes locked and I raised a hand in farewell, her smile was triumphant.

The Negotiation

How much for the car?

Which one?

The red Ford—the one with the dent in the left wing.

Scratch.

I beg your pardon?

Ain't no dent. That's a scratch.

It—ah—it looks like a pretty big dent to me … so?

So what?

How much is it? The red Ford.

Sixty thousand.

Sixty—! That's daylight robbery!

I ain't no thief.

You could be. Asking so much for a damaged vehicle. I may be an accountant, but I'm not made of money, you know. Where do you think I'll get that amount of cash from? My daughter's varsity tuition fees are due, and there's our holiday to France next month … I'll give you ten for it. Cash.

Sixty.

Absolutely not! … Fifteen. That's a very generous offer. No one else will give you that, not with that gouge out the front.

Scratch.

Gouge. It'll cost at least twenty thousand to repair.

Nope. Betsy, she got a quote on it, right after she dinged it. Ain't gonna cost much more than a couple o' hundred.

Betsy? Well, if this is Betsy's vehicle, I should be speaking to her. Perhaps she'll be more reasonable than you.

You cain't speak to Betsy.

Of course I cain … I mean, can. Where is she?

Betsy … my Betsy is with the Good Lord above. She passed two days after she made that scratch.

Oh … may she rest in peace … uh, when did she pass?

Thirty years ago, Mister. And the price is still sixty. Take it or leave it.

I'll leave it!

Thought you might.

Heroes' Day

I remember the full moon turning the night into day and the incessant hum of mosquitoes, interspersed with a sudden slap and a curse. I remember the sweat dribbling down my neck and the hushed murmurs of Bravo Company sliding through the hot still air.

Mostly I remember Pete.

He'd stepped off the Flossie that morning looking unbelievably young, and yet there was only a single year between us. Friends since we were *laaities*, I became his hero on the day we started junior school.

His glasses, and his small fragile build, gave him the look of a girl. The other boys, especially the jocks, thought they'd found the perfect victim and flicked his forearm with their wet towels until he had a *lammie* the size of a golf ball. But because I was so much bigger and tougher than him, Ma had made me promise to look after him so Pete's Ma—her best friend—wouldn't worry.

So I did and those *doff* jocks never bothered him again.

He became my shadow after that.

Even now, deep in the Angolan bush and crouched low in this godforsaken TB about forty clicks north of the border at Rundu, he's at my side.

The Flossie that brought him hadn't even cooled down before the Colonel was asking for volunteers. I'd lost four troops on my last search-and-destroy, and I had to go back over the border. Pete's hand shot up and I groaned because, as I'd discovered over the years, that slight body contained a will of steel.

"You're a rookie, Pete," I pleaded later, as I tore open the rat packs and stuffed the useful items into my chest webbing. "You haven't even been blooded."

He took a long draw on a Marlboro. I'd smoked them since I was thirteen, but this was the first time I'd seen him draw on one. Flicking the *stompie* into the gritty sand that had a way of creeping into everything in the camp, he dropped his foot from the wheel of the Ratel and straightened. "Nigel," he said. "You were a rookie once ... now you're a hero."

"I'm no hero," I muttered. "I'm just an old soldier. While you were being a bookworm at that fancy varsity of yours, I was learning to eat mopani worms to keep alive."

Ignoring his chuckle, I grabbed his arm. “I’ll square it with the Colonel. Just stay behind on this trip.”

“Nope,” he grinned. “I’m coming.” The steel was still there and I knew I wouldn't change his mind.

How could I tell him of the shiver that racked me, even in this intense heat? I said nothing when he shook me off. Pete was no coward and I could not turn him into one.

And so here we were. Together again, in the dark. But this time the silence wasn’t broken by soft moans as I kissed my first girl—Pete’s sister—in the back seat of my Dad’s car, while Pete kept watch to make sure none of the parents came out to see what we were doing.

This time the silence was broken by an eerie chanting, like the spirits of the dead yet to be, from the nearby village that was our morning target.

#

I zigzagged low over the chana. With a quick hand signal, I ordered the attack on the kraal. As swift as a swarm of ants, we breeched the walls. The Recces had done their job. The village was awash with the enemy. A boy, his black head shaved, hunched over a fire, casually stirring breakfast. When he saw us, he half stood. His familiar grey uniform with its distinctive red-and-brown rice flecks flapped as he tried to warn his comrades.

Without thought, I revved him. The *rat-a-tat-tat* blew him backwards. The potjie he was stirring crashed over, the fire hissing and spitting. A fat old pig rooting near the door of his hut snuffled in the half-cooked mess. Shouts and screams came from both the terrified villagers and the enemy soldiers. They flung themselves to the ground, caught between the gunfire and the grenades. I couldn’t tell which was enemy fire and which was ours.

They had no hope of survival, though. We were too thorough. Soon the shots faded and the smell of death and fear hung heavy over the kraal as I took roll call.

“Sikole?”

“Present.”

“Thabo?”

“Present.”

“Van der Poel?”

Silence. Then another voice shouted, "He's wounded, Kaptein, but alive."

I breathed again after each name was accounted for.

"Pete?" I called at last, and waited, filled with a new kind of fear. "Pete!"

"He's over there, Kaptein," the loot said.

Looking over my shoulder, I saw Pete. His face, white against the smudges of smoke and black-is-beautiful camo cream, was frozen. He stared at the young terr I'd shot first. My bullets had torn the terr's arm to pieces, an easy meal for the pig, tugging and snorting, so that his arm jumped and jerked, almost alive ... and then something in the lay of the body, a twitch in a cheek that should have been dead, warned me.

"Pete!" I shouted. My boots gripped the sand hard as I forced myself to run.

I was too late.

The body rolled over and up. Before I could say "He's alive!" the boy grabbed his fallen AK47 and yelled, "*A luta continua!*" Then he blasted a stream of bullets that had Pete dancing with macabre grace.

They say I screamed and swore and reloaded twice before they brought me down and stopped me shooting at that murderous *kaffir*.

All I remember is looking up from the ground, tasting dirt and the salt of sweat or tears. I watched as that fat old pig trotted eagerly over to where Pete's body lay and began to feast on his brains, seeping slowly from his shattered skull, staining the dirt of that foreign land where his bones still rest today.

Heroes' Day *first appeared in ITCH magazine, an online periodical published by the University of the Witwatersrand's School of Literature, Language and Media (South Africa) in March 2011.*

The Fan

The muggy heat is everywhere, even in the fridge, which no longer spews cold air when she opens it, only a tepid mist. A drop of sweat meanders slowly down her back. She shifts uncomfortably in the chair.

"Shall I switch the fan on?" The heat has sucked the energy from her husband's voice. "It's getting hotter."

She grunts a reply; it's too hot to say more.

With a sigh of effort, Jack slides off his chair, his open shirt flapping briefly against his paunch, shiny with perspiration. The click is loud in the oppressive room. The rustle of a page turning is a welcome sound, an indication of the first faint breeze pushing away the heavy heat. The fan gathers momentum, the whack-whack of its blades bringing a sigh of relief to her lips.

"Switch it higher," she says.

The lazy clacking drowns out the clink of her iced drink as she lifts it to cool her face. She lies back, closing out the sight of Jack spreading his bulk on the other couch, his bare toes stretching long and wide in ecstasy.

And the blurring blades slice through the heat as if it were a paltry thing.

Umbrella in the Snow

Still perfectly elegant after all these years, she never leaves home without it.

"It'll protect you," her daddy said, "when I can't."

"I'll treasure it forever, Daddy."

The earnest echo of her six-year-old self curves a smile on her face, smoothing the wrinkles guarding her narrow lips. Her heart warms at the memory of his booming voice. Forty years on—with him dead in his grave the past ten—she can make his vibrant voice manifest in an instant.

"I kept my promise, Daddy," she murmurs.

The taxi driver slews a puzzled glance over his shoulder. Pretending she'd said nothing, she looks out of the taxi, surprised at the flurry of snow beating densely against the window.

"Will we get there on time?"

"Sure," the driver confirms laconically, "as long as the storm stays away."

Relaxing, she leans back into the cracked leather seat. Snowstorms hold no fear for her, for they never touch her. The umbrella always keeps her safe.

Unknowingly her hand reaches out, seeking the strong steel handle. Colder than usual in the freezing weather, still it comforts her as she pulls it onto her lap, in much the same way her daddy had done to her. Her palm cuddles the familiar shape.

Perfect. It's perfect. The best umbrella anyone could ever have.

"One of a kind, Princess, just like you," Daddy said, as he'd helped her open it for the first time.

She'd tossed her thick plait of black hair over her shoulder, her eyes glowing. Inside—where it counted—she was a Princess. With her beautiful umbrella in her hand, everyone at school would see it too.

But the children in the playground only sniggered at the contrast the umbrella made against her shabby clothes. "Look at Naledi," they laughed. "She's barefoot again!"

She regally ignored them. Despite their amusement, she knew she was more special than they were.

With a flick of her wrist, the umbrella opened and she was safe. Safe from their coarseness. Safe from their vulgar minds that saw her only as the daughter of a lowly toilet paper salesman and not the one-of-a-kind princess she was.

Eventually, though, she convinced them. The way she spoke; the lift of her chin when displeased. She made sure every action reflected the inner majesty she saw in the mirror each day.

Soon people began to treat her with the respect she deserved. The girls stopped giggling when she walked by. The boys still kept their distance. Her beauty and her intelligence—the aura of dignity she surrounded herself with—were too good for the simple government school she attended.

Her daddy agreed.

"I'll be chief salesman soon," he promised. "Then you'll go to a proper school. One that teaches only the daughters of princes and presidents."

"Like me, Daddy?"

"Like you, Princess!"

She tensed with disappointment as her mother asked, "What about the washing machine you promised to buy me with the extra money?"

"That can wait," Daddy said. "Naledi's future is more important."

When the girls at her new school, who were no different to the ignorant children from the townships, laughed at her badly pronounced words, she simply opened the umbrella. It hid them from view until her elocution lessons polished everything but rounded vowels and clipped consonants from her speech. Slowly they, too, come to recognise she was one of them.

She fitted right in, as she'd known she would.

Moreover, rich girls have brothers. Soon she met her prince.

"You're extraordinarily gorgeous," he said. "One of a kind." Like Daddy, Mandla saw exactly who she was.

She married him.

The rounded vowels came more easily. Eventually she couldn't remember a time when she hadn't spoken with the biting edge of her new crystal voice.

She learnt, too, that with a trust fund behind her, it was easy to forget what being poor was like.

"High ideals are another privilege of the rich," her mother often said. "You've time to think, because you're not worrying about where the next meal for your children will come from. Or," she looked at the dirty shirt in her chafed hands, "doing the washing and ironing."

"Nonsense!" Sometimes her mother irritated her beyond belief. "You enjoy what you do."

"Only because I have to." Her mother looked at her bleakly. "We're still paying off your school fees."

Some truths one could only ignore. Silence reigned, until she asked, "What's happening in the village?"

"Lungihoek Primary is having their reunion. Are you going?"

"No."

"They were your friends, once," her mother—or her conscience—said. "You'll be sorry."

A twist of the umbrella blotted her out, and Naledi returned to her place at Mandla's side.

Her life became better and better. She hardly needed the umbrella at all, until recently.

"We need to talk, Naledi. Really talk—from our hearts."

"Later, Mandla," she said, again and again.

When he insisted, she fancied his voice leaving jagged footprints in clean, crisp snow. She poked him gently, almost affectionately, with the tip of the umbrella. "Rather tell me about your day."

With a sigh, knowing he couldn't fight the strength of the umbrella, he did. The flurries inside her subsided again, leaving her calm and still, hunched under the safety of the umbrella's arc.

Sometimes she thinks the snowstorms are coming closer and closer. Like the storm gathering ominously outside the taxi. A wave of unexpected heat engulfs her, making her clutch the umbrella tighter.

"Turn down the heater," she orders. "It'll melt the snow and make me filthy."

The click is loud in the small interior. She shivers gratefully. The cool air surrounding her makes it easier to think about The Telephone Call.

"Is that Naledi?"

The woman sounded vaguely familiar. Perhaps one of Mandla's secretaries, for she could never tell them apart.

"Yes," she'd said, dragging the word out with flawless diction. She doesn't enjoy being on first name terms with employees.

"Mandla wants a divorce. He says he can't talk to you."

The sudden hiss of an approaching snowstorm drowned out the woman's words.

"You say Mandla wants to talk to me?" Why would Mandla get some strange woman to tell her that?

"Go to the Hilton tonight. Be there at eight." The phone had clacked down in her ear and, replacing her handset, a slow smile had pulled up the habitual droop of her mouth. How romantic! She sighed dreamily. After all these years, my Prince is setting up a secret tryst.

The moan of the storm stopped as suddenly as it started.

Excited in a way she hadn't been for years, she primped, preened, and powdered herself. Looking at the result in the mirror, she'd congratulated herself on how much she'd achieved in her life.

A happy home, in the best suburb in the north. Two children, educated at the best schools, grown now, and happily climbing the ranks in their father's business. Exciting events to fill her days with activities once out of reach for people like her: tennis on Mondays, movies with friends on Tuesdays, Wednesdays she works for Mandla from the computer in their home study. And so her weeks, and her life, went on.

At times, when the winter blues brought the snowstorms ever closer, raising goosebumps of unknown fears on her skin, she'd wondered if her life was too happy. Can life be too happy? But, safe under the haven of her umbrella, she'd stop worrying and the whiteout would always fade away.

This one, she notes, with another glance at the driving snow, is taking a while to pass by. The taxi driver, his untrimmed moustache reminding her of a dense, unexplored forest, is as unconcerned as ever.

"I'll get you there, lady," he promises. What has he seen in her expression? "Look," he adds, pointing with two fingers, a stubby, ash-tipped cigarette between them. "There's your hotel."

He's pleasant, she decides, despite the shabby appearance. Perhaps he only needs some of her guidance. "Smoking's unhealthy for you. You should give it up."

She can't be sure, but she thinks he looks annoyed.

"We all have our weaknesses, lady." He pauses, briefly capturing her eyes in the mirror. "At least mine bring me pleasure."

Is that a warning? She frowns, and then starts as a gust of snow hammers the small taxi, dragging her thoughts away from his odd reply.

"You should try to overcome your weaknesses," she urges.

"*Eish*! You're one of a kind, lady, you know?"

She smiles imperially at him, pleased, and surprised, that he has the intelligence to recognise what she is. Not approving the habit of giving gratuities to people who, when serving her, are only doing their jobs, she decides to add a small tip to his fare.

"We're here," he says, opening the door for her. Sometime during their conversation, they must have passed through the last of the storm, for there is nothing but clear, crisp snow lying all around.

With all the grace her long-ago dancing lessons instilled in her, she climbs out, nodding her thanks.

Casually tapping his forehead with two fingers, he says, "Good luck," and laughs as he disappears, his final words drifting back at her. "You'll need it."

What an odd man, she decides, dismissing him from her mind as she searches the foyer for Mandla.

She sees him, coming out of the bar.

"Mandla," she calls, "I'm here."

He swings his face toward her. Instead of the smile she expects to see—the familiar, slow smile he'd given her when they were first in love—his face clenches with an indescribable agony.

"Mandla!" She rushes to his side, thinking heart attack! Her own heart thumps loudly in her chest.

"What are you doing here, Naledi?"

The relief that he is well barely allows for curiosity.

"You invited me to dinner," she replies.

He shakes his head, the streaks of grey softening the black curls cupping his head more attractively than ever. "It wasn't me," he denies, turning his head away from her.

Only then does she see the young woman standing next to him, her hand, smooth and unwrinkled, lying possessively on his arm.

"I invited her," the young woman says. A pleading note enters her voice as she looks up at Mandla. "It's time she knew about us."

"Mandla ...?"

"Naledi, are you all right?"

Of course, I'm all right, she wants to say. I'll be fine, just fine: as soon as I open my umbrella. Then she can apologise for interrupting his business dinner. She'll return home, grabbing a quick bite of leftovers from the fridge. She'll wait for him to come and, as usual, tell her about his day.

"I ... I ..." Her hands struggle with the umbrella. "J-just let me ..." Her voice breaks on a sob as the umbrella refuses to open. "What am I going to do," she cries, "without my umbrella?"

"Naledi ..." Guilty exasperation laces his deep voice. "There *is* no umbrella."

She ignores him, jerking and tugging the worn catch. For the first time ever, the umbrella refuses to open.

"Mad old cow," she hears the young woman say, her voice faint in the soft sibilance of the returning storm. "No wonder you want to divorce her."

Mandla's reply is lost ... lost as her umbrella as she falls, deep into the banks of melting snow, drowning, drowning, in her old nightmare.

She isn't, after all, one of kind. Like so many other souls on this earth, she is simply an ordinary woman.

An ordinary woman: alone and unloved, without even an umbrella to keep her safe.

Umbrella in the Snow *first appeared in ITCH magazine, an online periodical published by the University of the Witwatersrand's School of Literature, Language and Media (South Africa) in May 2013.*

A Dish Best Eaten Cold

I've never picked up a man before. He catches my interest by reading aloud from the newspaper, to anyone who will listen at the restaurant bar.

"If I have anything to say about it," (which he does, at length), "Men will stay strong and women will stay ... feminine."

He's seen my secret smile at that, and hooks into it as an invitation to move the spidery barstool closer, the imitation red leather squeaking as he slides into a more comfortable position. The silky nylon sheen of my legs fascinates him as I bend down to move my handbag, allowing him to shift even nearer.

"Don't you agree?" he asks, turning the full voltage of his smile to me. "Look at this rubbish," he says, hitting the photograph in the paper so hard his thick gold bracelet jingles amongst the curly black hair erupting from his hands and arms, a proud symbol of his potency. "A woman's soul in a man's body? *Wat die fok* is that?"

Not wanting or expecting an answer, he makes a rude sound with his lips. I watch with morbid fascination as they curl wetly around his next words.

"A sports star one day, a homemaker the next!" Softening his indignant roar (in case I think he's putting us women down), he pats my knee benignly. "Not that there's anything wrong with cooking and cleaning and," he waves a helpless hand towards the restaurant kitchen, "all that, it's okay for a pretty little woman like you. But it's not natural that a man goes in for this operation thing—" slashing the air, he grimaces as he cuts off an imaginary penis, "—and comes out of hospital preferring dresses. *Blerrie moffie!*"

"He was such a little man," I say and look, with mixed feelings, at the photograph showing a small, blond man proudly wearing the No 9 scrum half jersey in the green and gold colours of the national squad. "Maybe that accounts for it."

"Nonsense," he booms in reply, softening the blow to my frail feminine feelings with another pat.

I give him a soft smile, which swells his chest and adds a hint of obscure lust to the corners of his mouth. Some imp within me makes me put my hand on his arm to let him know I understand. We both look down, intrigued by the vermilion red of my nails shining more brightly than before as they lie on his forearm, gently crushing that dark pelt.

“It’s not a problem, though, is it?” I ask with deadpan concern. “We women are lucky to still have some real men around.” I give him a significant look.

His lips relax, and he covers my hand with his, swallowing it up; leaving me with a sense of helplessness in the face of such an awesome, virile confidence, something I’ve always been a stranger to. Taking my hand to his lips in a gesture he copies from some long-forgotten movie, he kisses my fingers before standing up eagerly, tall in the knowledge that he has reached a good decision for both of us.

“Let me buy you dinner,” he declares. “We’ll carry on talking about this over a good plate of food.”

I hesitate briefly. How far should I take this? I ask myself.

I give in to my baser instincts. It’s clear he finds me attractive; there’s a little gleam that makes his eyes seem feral, and I find myself nodding a quick agreement. Diminished by his height—I hardly reach his shoulder—I incline my head gracefully and ask, “Are you sure?”

Impossible as it seems, his confidence grows with every second. “My pleasure,” he says and puts his arm around my shoulder, giving me a squeeze just firm enough to allow me to enjoy the potential of his rugged chest as he leads me away from the bar.

Planting his feet wide, he stares around the restaurant until a waiter oozes over to show us to our seats. Whipping the serviette off the table, the waiter lays it on my lap with a playful flourish. Complimenting me on my dress (his eyes leave an invisible trail as they slide across the plumpness of my breasts) he almost makes me blush with pleasure. His admiration makes my companion preen, a consort in pleasure.

Our drinks eventually arrive: Schaapenberg Sauvignon Blanc for me and a rich Nederberg Merlot for him. I forget for a moment and nod to the waiter to pour.

My companion tut-tuts and says, “Let me do that.”

Feeling oddly incompetent I sit back, annoying myself with the thanks I give, which somehow reinforce his opinion that it’s a chore only he can do.

“Funny, hey,” he says, lifting the wine from the ice bucket and twisting the screw cap open. “It was his favourite wine too.”

My eyes follow the cascading wine, separated from the domination of his fingers by only a thin glass he could easily crush.

"Who's favourite?' I ask, well knowing the answer, but wanting to hear what he says. Idly, I wonder if he would crush the glass if I asked him to. Would I enjoy the display as much as he would enjoy impressing me? The pale yellow stream stops too soon and he hands me the glass before I can give in to the temptation of seeing how far he will go.

"That *moffie*, Leslie Watson! He had us all fooled, hey!" he marvels. "We should have known from his name—Leslie, with an 'i'!" Tossing back his drink in one mighty gulp to show his disdain for such a heretical name (for a sports star), he continues his diatribe. "What a waste! The man was the best scrum half I ever saw," shaking his head at the loss. It's as if he takes it personally.

What, I reflect, *did Leslie Watson ever do to him?*

"He even played for my club," making the sacrilege of Leslie Watson's crime clearer. "And both he and his Pa played in the Nationals." Another unforgivable betrayal of the brotherhood of real men. "If he ... she ... *fok*, whatever, felt he wasn't a man, why did he play sport?"

When I remain silent, lost in a melancholy I can't avoid, he gives me an approving nod and provides the answer himself. "I'll tell you why. Because then we would've known what he was. This way," he adds with a strange little hitch in his voice, "he could jerk off in the change room. Must have been better than one of those gay porno mags for him, seeing us all there like that—in the raw! Nude," he adds, in case I didn't get the message the first time.

And there, beneath the noble indignation for his sports mates, I hear the current of fear swirling into unspeakable thoughts as he wonders *did I do anything in the change room to let Leslie Watson think he could fuck me?*

Even worse, *does that make me a faggot too?*

I understand, now, the unthinkable threat the apostate Leslie Watson posed to the *esprit de sports corps*. I find it hard to hide my sympathy. Shifting uncomfortably in my seat, I think: I shouldn't have started this.

It's too late now. So, not knowing why I feel like this, I try to make it easier for him as I say gently, "Maybe there was another reason."

"What?" he asks, ready to indulge me.

Petulantly moving my leg away from his oppressive hand, which suddenly annoys me, I shrug as casually as I can and say, "Could be he's just tired of pretending to be something he's not." Covering my irritation, which is gone almost as quickly as it came, I direct a fragile smile at him. "I've had enough. Let's get out of here into the fresh air."

Visions of hotel rooms dance before his eyes, and he imperiously calls our waiter across. Full of brotherly camaraderie (tinged with envy at his luck), the waiter energetically arranges for the bill to be presented. The platinum card accurately flashes its stature at me; I raise a delicately plucked brow in acknowledgment.

Then we're walking towards the exit, our waiter beaming his approval as he says, "Have a good night, sir. Come again soon, sir." Before he would have greeted me, but now it's as if I'm lost in the shadow of the man beside me.

He walks slightly behind me, carefully holding his coat low in front of him, his hand at my elbow tenderly guiding my way. I can't help myself; I let my hips loosen into that peculiar sway that only a woman who has been made aware of her own desirability can achieve. He sees it too, and his hand drops from my elbow to the hollow in my back as he pulls me nearer until our hips clash with every step we take.

As he courteously helps me into the taxi, his hot hand with its muscular fingers eagerly slides up my leg. I listen to his voice, husky with anticipated pleasure, as it whispers in my ear, "Pretty little lady, you never did get to tell me your name."

"It's Leslie," I say quietly, "Leslie with an 'i'," and I leave him, there on the sidewalk, with only his thoughts and his hard-on for company.

Coming Home

The old white Citroën was the only car that stopped as, clutching my small cow-skin bag, I trudged along the highway between Nairobi and home.

Looking at the missing front passenger door and the breathing bodies and smelly shoes packed into every possible nook and cranny in the car, I thought it was a fitting penance for a renegade bishop cast aside by his Church.

The rosary, hanging haphazardly from the rear view mirror, was probably the reason the driver stopped when he saw my sombre black suit, frayed dog collar and the crucifix glittering in the rising sun.

What would they say, these loyal sheep of my ex-flock, if they knew I no longer had a right to the collar and no longer believed in the golden symbol of a white man's faith?

"*Habari ya asubuhi,* Father!" the driver greeted me. "*Habari yako?*"

"*Habari,*" I replied and, although I was anything but fine, I answered his polite enquiry, "*Nzuri, asante.*"

"Where are you going?"

"Isiolo."

"*Ai, Ai, Ai!*" A toothless old man, squashed between a clutch of chickens and a young woman holding her whimpering baby, spoke. "God must give his priests extra-strong soles on their shoes to walk such a distance!"

Too tired to do more, I waited for the laughter to die down, and then asked, "Will you save this priest's soles?" I lifted my foot, the one with the sole of the shoe worn through.

More cackles from the old man, which startled the chickens into a raucous chorus. He jerked a thumb upwards. "You can ride up there."

There wasn't even space on the roof for another pair of shoes, let alone my portly shape. My heart quailed. In the years of my priesthood, I'd become too used to the comforts of my office.

Tightening my grip on my sack as I reached for the roof rack, I used the empty door space as a step and, with a few friendly prods from below, landed on the bed of shoes. Shifting into a more comfortable position, I pulled an old leather sandal out of my ribs. With its toecap cut away for a pair of feet a size too big, it—like my crucifix and I—offered only a dignity that didn't quite fit.

My seat was precarious but, without complaint, I sat amongst the shoes for kilometre after dusty kilometre as the car chugged along, coughing and popping. Under the hot sun, surrounded by smells and memories of five hundred different pairs of feet, I drifted into a half-sleep.

How hard Mama had worked to send me to the Sacred Heart Secondary School. How proud she had been, ululating and dancing, as I caught that first bus to the seminary. I returned less and less often as—carried by Mama's faith and my ambition to escape the poverty of my childhood—I'd risen through the hierarchy of the church. But each time I'd climbed off the Nairobi bus, Mama had been waiting, insisting I never take my dog collar off.

"This is my son," she'd say, "the Priest." The day she'd first said, "This is my son, the Bishop," she'd cried with pride.

Where had those days gone?

And what would Mama say this time I came home?

The wind and the dust out there on the top of the car roof made my eyes water. I didn't bother to wipe them, for who but God could see the wetness on my cheeks as other memories crowded in the shade of Mama's joy?

As the sun climbed the sky, Thika Road wound its steady way north and we drove past the village of Naro Moru just as the last of the morning clouds swirled around Mount Kenya. I stared at the jagged peaks and their retreating glaciers. No wonder, I thought, the Kikuyu believe this sacred mountain is the home of *Ngai*, but where would their God go when the last of the ice has melted?

The passing terrain became drier and dustier and, after the tar road had turned abruptly into sand, the old Citroën finally clunked to a halt. Accompanied by a shoe or two, I clambered down to the solid earth of Isiolo and stretched my aching bones.

"Did you find a new pair of shoes, Father?" the old man asked, smacking his toothless gums together as he laughed at my dishevelment. The young woman with the baby shushed him and, grabbing my hand, entreated, "Bless me, Father, and wish my son a long life!"

I hesitated, wanting to say no. But those dark brown eyes, set in a face too young for the wrinkles the sun and poverty had inscribed across it, stopped my refusal.

My hand squeezed tightly on the brown-and-white cow-skin sack I carried. No one heard the faint rattle it made as I raised my hand and muttered the prayer that now sounded so odd on my lips.

I waited until the brown dust the car kicked up swirled into nothingness. Ignoring the giant blue mural of a white Jesus Christ staring down at me, I stripped off the foreign clothes that had defined me for so long. Then I untied the knot on my sack, inhaling the scents of the sacred herbs and potions lying amongst the traditional dress of the *mugwe.*

When she saw me, Mama would cry and call me a witchman. But, as I knotted the beaded red cloth across my shoulders and took out the small calabash, with its goat's bones and bottle tops, buttons and shells, I could feel no sorrow.

I lifted my face and, rattling the calabash at the African sun burning with fierce pride on my bare skin, I began to chant.

"*Mizimu*," I called to my ancestors. "I am home!"

Flash Fiction I

Clouds in the Sky

Wisps of white sails;
Souls on a journey.
Stark arms, far below,
Cry out. Reach out.
The wind skitters
Across the heavenly blue sky,
All is swept away.

Sunset on the Ranch

Red walls. White rain falls
On sunlit mountains rising
Over the homestead.

Abandon Ship

Battered and torn,
A sandy skeleton leaves
Memories of life.

Letting Go

a water droplet
oozes along the safety of the leaf
until it cannot hold
rushing
into the silver lake.

Black Waters

"There!" she thought with a small, secret smile, "that wasn't so difficult after all!"

Tucking the last strand of her greying hair under her swimming cap, Victoria allowed herself to feel discreetly satisfied with the way dinner had gone the night before.

At last, her adored son would be free from that stupid girl he'd married over two years ago. No man, not even one as blinded by love as Kevin was, could accept the thought of his wife having an affair. Her chin lifting slightly, she pursed her lips into a tight half-smile as she thought of Susan, her daughter-in-law. She knew it was her inviolable duty as a mother to save him from *that woman.* But, even after last night, she still had difficulty believing that Susan had made it so easy for her.

Surprisingly though, Kevin had not seemed as angry as she had expected. What if she'd been wrong? Shaking her head to clear that faint ripple of anxiety—she could never be wrong, especially where her beloved son was concerned—Victoria swiftly completed the preparations for her daily swim.

As she had for the past forty years, she ran her hands down her still slim, wiry body admiring her chic appearance even in something as simple as a swimsuit. Smiling at her reflection, she scooped up her towel and strolled out of the sliding glass door, down to the secluded beach where she spent the first hour of every morning, hoping that today Wilson, the family housekeeper, would not forget to bring her iced tea to the beach. Quietly humming the first few bars of *My Way*, she let her towel slip to the sand and waded into the brooding water to begin her morning exercise.

#

Deep in thought, Kevin stood slightly hunched as usual and looked unseeingly out of the window at the flat turquoise sea. He'd never understand women, especially his mother. Would she never know how much he loved her? Would she never be secure enough to accept he could love Susan too without loving her less? Despite her neediness, he knew his mother loved him in her way. At times though, like last night, she demanded too much from his love for her.

Victoria had waited until the coffee was served. "Who was that divine looking man I saw you having lunch with today, Susan dear?" she'd said, speaking to Susan but looking at him. "You and your friend looked so … friendly I didn't want to disturb you."

Susan had jumped, her knife and fork clattering onto the best china plates his mother insisted on using every night, as she'd stuttered, "W-w-which man, Victoria?"

"This one!" his mother had said, pulling out her cellphone and waving the screen in Kevin's direction. To make her happy, he'd looked at it and seen Susan, smiling, relaxed, sitting close to a young handsome man, papers and coffee cups spread out before them.

Kevin frowned as he thought of his poor, sensitive Susan. She'd flushed a pale pink, lowered her eyes and mumbled something unintelligible.

Assured of Susan's guilt, his mother's nostrils had flared with elation. "My boy," she'd said, so earnest in her purpose she couldn't even hear the triumphant malice in her own voice, "I hope Susan realises how lucky she is having a husband as liberal as you are. Not many young husbands would have such an open mind." Her firm chin, always at odds with her relentless civility, lifted higher, the corners of her mouth tightly downturned with disapproval.

Turning to Susan again, she'd continued in a voice made breathless with victory. "Dear child, take advice from one who knows better than you. It's not wise for young wives with your background to be unappreciative of their husbands. Who knows what might happen?" She'd stretched out a polite smile that barely deepened the lines around her eyes as they'd flicked over Susan. Then she'd poked at her phone and he'd heard the ping of an incoming message. "There! I've sent Kevin the picture, in case he needs it." Finally satisfied, she'd sat back and elegantly wiped the last traces of coffee from her lips.

Susan's reaction had frightened him and he'd known then that he'd almost left it too late. His wife was so different to him: fire red to his ice blue. Bubbling with tempestuous warmth, filling his life with a joy never experienced during a boyhood that was disciplined, reserved and so proper at times he'd wanted to scream, his wife was as foreign to his mother as a lion was to London.

Usually after one of the regular skirmishes with Victoria, she'd passionately weep for hours and then, for his sake, hide her hurt behind a watery smile. Last night had been different.

Susan had seemed so calm and placid; so untouched by Victoria's attack that he'd been unable to suppress a sudden feeling of dread.

If Susan left him there'd be a void in his life that no other woman could fill. His mother had nominated him as the man in her life ever since his father had died twenty years ago, but the time had come for her to know that what she saw as a terrible mistake, he saw as his saving grace. While he loved her as much as any son loved his mother, he was his own man now: a man with a wife, and he would no longer sit by watching Victoria destroy that which he cherished most.

He had not told her of his plans to move out of the family home, hoping to avoid the inevitable recriminations. How was she to know that the man Susan had been having lunch with the day before was an estate agent? If she was so eager to see only bad in Susan, how far would she go to claw back her position in his life as his 'No 1 woman'?

At the sound of a commotion outside, Kevin gratefully roused himself from his dark reverie. As a dishevelled and frightened Wilson ran into the room, Kevin felt the same sense of dread that had alarmed him the previous night constrict his heart.

During ten years of service, even in dire circumstances, the prim Wilson had never walked at a pace faster than that of a stately turtle.

"Kevin! Sir!" he gasped, clutching Kevin's arm with a shaking hand. "The beach … the madam ..." He broke off, unable to continue and in his distress he leaned against Kevin, who recoiled from the dampness of Wilson's usually pristine suit, covered in sand and sea water.

Kevin's first thought was, "Susan?" and his bottomless fear made him shake Wilson hard to calm him. "Where is my wife?"

Kevin's anxiety seemed to recall Wilson to a sense of his duty, and striving for equilibrium, he slowed his breathing, took a step back and, as he tugged his jacket straight, he said, "No, sir, not Miss Susan. It's Madam Victoria. She … She …" His shaky voice belied his attempt at composure, "It appears, Sir, that Madam Victoria has drowned."

He looked at Wilson as if he was speaking in a language that he couldn't understand. Sorrow pushed through his body, turning his legs to water and tightening his throat. Every ounce of will power went into keeping his voice steady as he asked, "Are you sure?"

Turning away from Wilson's slow nod he drew in a deep breath. He looked at the serene waters his mother had swum in for over forty years and felt a surge of anger towards its deceptive beauty, followed by an overwhelming yearning for Susan. He needed her now more than ever; he wanted her vitality to give him the strength he required to face what was waiting for him on the beach.

As if she answered his unspoken call, Susan walked into the room enquiring what all the excitement was about. At the sight of her he brokenly murmured "Sue! Sue! Mother's dead, she's drowned."

The harsh reality of the words was sufficient to snap his iron control and, covering his quivering mouth with his shaking hand, he turned to her.

Taking him into her arms, Susan reflected on a future without her meddlesome mother-in-law. As she soothed and comforted her husband, she shook back her hair, still damp from the sea, and pondered how Victoria, a creature of habit, had made it so easy for her.

"There!" she thought with a small, secret smile, "that wasn't so difficult after all!"

Whispers of Love

She wears a black-and-white dress when first I meet her. There's not much of it, but on her, it looks good. I'm old—seventy next birthday—and married, but I'm not dead yet, and so I look at her legs. She sees me looking, and smiles; a smile far too full of ancient knowledge for one so young.

"Do you play?" she asks, with a graceful gesture towards the giant chessboard. Painstakingly woven into the paving of the square in front of the city's library, it nestles beneath a clump of birch trees.

I come to the square every day. It keeps me busy and my wife happy.

"I've had the house to myself for twenty years since the kids left," my wife said, five years ago on the first day of my retirement. She pressed my old work lunchbox into my hand, laughing. "I wouldn't know what to do with you around here all day. Go, play your chess! Make new friends! I'll see you later."

And so I go. Monday to Friday, the same discipline that dragged me through my office routine for all those years gets me to the square at nine, sharp. Sometimes, I talk to the others, or I sit and read in the library; other times I play chess, if there's a newcomer to the square willing to play me.

Then she is there, with her chessboard dress and her frighteningly wise smile, on the same day the feathery twigs of the delicate birches burst forth with the spring's new buds.

"Do you play?" she asks again.

"Sometimes," I say. "If I can find a challenger."

She looks around the scattered benches, mostly full of men like me, too old to be of any real use to anyone, but not yet ready to die. We gather here, flexing the muscles of our fading power by testing each other in games at which there's only ever one winner.

"You've got plenty of opponents here," she says.

I shrug, and say nothing. Old Tony—the reigning champion until I came along—says, "No one plays Jeremy, Missie." He sniggers, his false teeth clattering in his toothless gums. "There are no fools here."

She looks at me speculatively. “You’re good.”

“Some say so.” I shrug off the compliment, but can’t hide the small smile of pride, the privilege of victory.

“My name’s Charlie,” she says. “I’ll take black.”

She must be sure of herself, for no one gives me the opening move. But, despite her wise old eyes, she’s young, and pretty. I rein in my predatory instincts and say kindly, “Take white.”

She doesn’t answer; her long, bare legs stride decisively to the black pawns. “Your move,” she says, and looks me straight in the eye.

My blood heats at her challenge, but I keep my face impassive. “Best of three?” I ask. A gentleman, I’ll let her win the first game, and then I can, in clear conscience, play as I always do: to win.

Old Tony and crew hoot at my familiar question. Her eyes flicker and, still as a cat on the prowl, I watch her weigh up the offer. Finally, she nods and I move my King’s pawn, the thrill of the hunt rich and thick in my heart ...

She’s back the next day and, as she enters the square, I reveal my eagerness by jumping to my feet. Warmth steals into my cheeks at Old Tony’s chortling. He was laughing when he left yesterday, and when he arrived this morning. He probably fell asleep laughing. “Now you know what it’s like,” he says, stroking his mangy beard, his knuckles gnarled with age and arthritis. “The taste of defeat.”

I ignore him. I see only her, heading straight for me with her distinctive stride.

“I’ll take black,” she says again, by way of greeting. “Best of three?”

I nod grimly, and make my move. Today, I play every game only to win.

As the spring buds unfurl into heart-shaped leaves and the catkins ripen into juicy brown fruit, the girl continues to beat me as we play our game under the feathery shade of the birches.

“Slow down,” my wife says over breakfast one Friday morning near the end of that summer. “You’ll get indigestion if you eat so fast.”

“I’ve got an important match today,” I mumble into my coffee. She still thinks I’m the local champion, but I haven’t won a match since Charlie came.

I slam my half-full cup on the table, a wave of bitter coffee sloshing over the edge. “I’m going,” I say, even though the faded melamine kitchen clock, embossed with photos of our grandchildren, shows that it's not yet eight o'clock.

"I haven't seen you this eager to leave since you retired," my wife says, getting up from the table to swipe a cloth over the mess I made. "Is there a championship match on?"

"Yes," I lie. It's less humiliating than telling her I lose daily, three games in a row. Or that my opponent is a girl almost fifty years younger than I.

"Are you having some good matches?"

I have to agree, though it galls me. "The best I've ever played." Yet, I never beat the girl. My game improves daily, but she always wins, no matter what move I devise, what challenge I issue. Suddenly I need to share my frustration.

"I'm losing," I confess and unhook my coat, folding it over my arm. "Every game."

"What?" My wife stops her cleaning and her surprise is a balm to my wounded pride. "You're joking! You never lose." She looks at me, her eyes bright with surprise and her hands twisting in her apron, the old flowered one our daughter made years ago. "Aren't you?"

I shake my head.

"Good heavens. Who are you playing?"

"Charlie," I say.

"Charlie who?"

I drop my gaze and watch my hand pick invisible lint off my coat. When did my knuckles become as gnarled as Old Tony's? "Don't know," I mumbled. Other than her initial greeting, the girl never says anything except "Checkmate."

My wife persists. "Is he from around here?"

I don't correct her. It's enough she knows I'm no longer champion. "What does it matter?"

"It doesn't," she says and returns to her cleaning. But when I kiss her on my way out the door, she pats my cheek and says, "Good luck!"

There is a touch of autumn in the air and I huddle in my coat; the first golden leaves crunch beneath my boots as I cross the square. Old Tony is there, and all the others, the ones I beat with monotonous ease.

"Morning, Jeremy." Old Tony, of course. "Ready to lose ... again?" He almost chokes on his laugh. Only the quick action of one of his cronies prevents him from sliding off the smooth stone bench.

"I'll win today." Does anyone else hear the uncertainty hovering in the shadows of my confident declaration? I hope not, and settle down to wait, concentrating on the faded black-and-white figures, solemnly still until the girl and I give them life in our intimate little war.

Should I risk my rook? I wonder, as muted conversation slips around me.

<He'll win today. I'll put five on Jeremy to win.>

Or should I try a double attack to pin her knight?

<Nope. He's lost his edge. A tenner on Jeremy losing.>

What if, I think, I use my queen to ...?

"Jeremy."

Old Tony calls me, but I ignore him, not wanting to lose the shape of the battle plan I'm drawing up in my head. Intricate and unusual, she'll find it hard to beat.

"Jeremy!"

He's not going to go away. "What?" I say.

"It's late already. Who are you going to play today?"

A cursory glance around the square confirms that the girl is not there, and a faint desolation, a sense of abandonment, slips into me.

And yet ... some part of me, the scared and conceited part of me needing to win, is fiercely glad. Today, I know I won't lose.

I look at Old Tony. "You." I grin coldly. "I'll play you."

Fool that he is, he swaggers arthritically to stand by the white. He knows I play only the best, and he's proud I choose him.

I walk to stand by the black and the flurry of words takes shape, bets hissed back and forth. A few risk-takers lay long odds on Old Tony winning, but they haven't noticed how badly I need to win again.

"Your move," Old Tony says, shuffling back from heaving a stone pawn almost as tall as he is.

This is going to be so easy. I sigh. Too easy. And casually, almost carelessly, I make my move.

"Checkmate," I say a short while later. Old Tony slinks back to his bench, grateful for the consolation cup of coffee his cronies push into his hand, and a ripple runs through the crowd as they watch.

<I told you he's back on form! That's twenty you owe me.>

I relax at the praise, stretching my arms over my head to release the tension in my shoulders and a halo of blonde hair, shining alone at the edge of the crowd, catches my attention.

"Charlie!" My arms drop and I half smile at her, but her gaze slides away to rest on Old Tony, his crowing silenced by defeat. That full bottom lip, which I've sometimes imagined kissing when I cover my wife's familiar mouth with my own, trembles and my heart thumps with inexplicable sadness as I see the glint of moisture in her eyes.

"Charlie?" I call, and move towards her, but the backslapping congratulations hinder me. By the time I get to where she stood, not even the gentle smell of her perfume lingers. Why did she leave at my moment of triumph?

It's enough, I tell myself, that she saw what I'm capable of. She has seen the skill that made me the unbeaten champion for five long years, until she came. I turn my back on the emptiness she leaves behind, and push my way through the crowd.

Tomorrow, I promise myself, the fizz of victory powering my steps homewards, tomorrow, I'll be able to beat her—at last.

Not much changes, though, the next week and the next.

Except for Fridays when, no matter how long I delay, she never arrives until after I've started playing Old Tony, it's the girl who says, "Checkmate," three times in a row.

I always ask, "Will you be back tomorrow?"

"Perhaps," she says as she leaves, her hair a nimbus of silver-blonde in the sun falling on the square, warming the benches where Old Tony sits and crows at my defeat.

Throughout the autumn, as the birches become barer and the bark peels back like slivered paper, the only games I win are those I play on Fridays.

Each time, I watch Old Tony shrink until his cup of coffee—almost too heavy for his shaking hand to hold—is finished. Then I turn my eyes to where I know she stands, watching. But, no matter with what ruthless brilliance I win, she never smiles or acknowledges my victory.

"Charlie will only respect me," I say to my wife, "when I thump her."

There are no secrets now. My wife came to the square to watch us play. She never said a word about Charlie being young and female. I love her even more for that and, every day as I leave, she encourages me. "Do your best," she murmurs, "and win against Charlie today."

It helps, knowing at least one person still believes I can win a match against the girl. But the only person I beat with remorseless regularity is Old Tony.

I search the Internet; my wife buys me old, out-of-print books by past masters and I devour them in my search for some obscure move that will bring me the peace of saying "Checkmate, Charlie." The words have a sweet ring that I taste every night in my dreams. But I've yet to say them aloud in the square.

The only solace I find, and it's as weak as the coffee Old Tony drinks, is when I annihilate the old man. I play every game only to win, and to win as best I can. But when he sits sipping his after-match coffee, I wonder if I look as frail, every time Charlie beats me.

"Did you hear about Old Tony?" my wife asks one morning as she ladles hot oatmeal into my bowl.

"What about him?"

"He's dying."

I bark a laugh at her dour expression. "We all are! At eighty-nine, he's just closer to the grave then the rest of us." I add more milk to my oatmeal and say, "He'll outlive me."

"No," she says and shudders as the first winter winds rattle the window pane with eager fingers. "I mean, he's really dying. I saw his wife yesterday."

I finish chewing first, before I ask, "What's he got? The big C?"

She shakes her head, and toys with the sugar spoon, lifting it up and turning it over, again and again, the crystals streaming back into the bowl under her unsettled gaze.

"It's his heart," she says eventually.

"Not surprising at his age."

I swallow a few more mouthfuls in silence, until she sighs, and adds, "Shelley's asked me to speak to you about it."

"Me?" What does Old Tony's wife think I can do about his heart? In my old life, before I retired and became a chess champion, I was a lawyer, not a doctor.

A nervous glance, and then her eyes are back on the waterfall of sugar, rushing headlong off the edge of the spoon into the abyss that awaits each crystal. “She wants you to let Tony win.”

“*Let* him win?”

She sighs, and plunges the spoon into the sugar before pushing the bowl away. “Yes. Lose to Old Tony. Would that be so hard?”

“It would be damn well impossible,” I say blankly, not quite sure I understand her, yet knowing there can be no other meaning to her words. “The only person I’ve ever lost to is Charlie, and I’ll beat her soon.”

“Will you?” my wife says, and something in her eyes infuriates me.

“Yes,” I snarl. “I will.”

“That’s what’s killing Old Tony.”

“What?”

“Your pride.”

I look at her stupidly. Her lips crimp closed in frustration, and she rises, gathering the few breakfast dishes and piling them in the sink before turning to face me. She rests her backside—still pert enough, even at her age, to heat my loins—against the sink and says, “It’s only a chess game, Jeremy, but it’s all Old Tony has.”

“It’s all *I* have,” I say, “since I retired. There can only be one winner.”

She shakes her head. ‘There’s more than one way to win and what you’re doing to Old Tony isn’t winning.”

“It’s no less than what Charlie does to me every day.” I get up, the chair screeching my annoyance across the tiled kitchen floor. “You don’t hear me whining about it. I just get on with the job of finding a way to beat her.”

She shrugs, turning back to the dishes, opening the tap so the gush of water deadens her words. “It kills him a little more,” she says, “each time you win so completely.”

The conversation lingers with me for weeks, souring the joy I should feel every time I beat the old man. Somehow I can’t stop noticing how very old he’s looking: his hand trembles more and more; he burrows into his winter coat and his once-irritating laugh never rings out in the square anymore. And I remember the tears Charlie cried the first time she watched me thrash Old Tony.

There comes a day when, with his first move, the old man makes a fundamental error. I taste a glorious victory; it'll be so easy to crush him in moments.

Charlie has arrived by then, her bright hair uncovered even in the creeping cold. I meet her chill stare until Old Tony startles me as he cups his hands together with a loud clap, lifting them to his mouth and blowing them warm. I look closer at this man who has been a fixture in the square for as long as I've been coming. There's a look about him; in his fading eyes and the way he stands, diminished by the unrelenting size of the stone chessmen. My wife's voice whispers in my head, "He's dying."

Looking at him, I know she speaks the truth. Another whisper fills my head and it takes me a long, long while to make my move. An hour later, I say gruffly, "Congratulations, Tony." His proud grin beats the quiver of my dying pride into submission and I return it, adding, "I didn't see that move coming." He cackles gleefully. It's months since I heard him laugh in that particular way.

"I'm not in my grave yet, Jeremy," he says, tottering over to sit on his bench, lifting his face to the weak winter sun, his happiness smoothing out the highways of age that criss-cross his face.

The backslapping congratulations are all for Old Tony today. Soon, I stand alone ... except for Charlie. I try to smile at her but I can't bear her to see my loss so, today, I turn away first. A gentle touch on my arm stops me and I fall into blue, blue eyes framed by the angelic perfection of her face.

"You played well today, Jeremy," she says, her smile as bright as her hair. "The best I've ever seen you play." It's the first time she's called me by my name.

"I lost," I say blankly.

She touches a hand to my cheek. Her fingertips sear a path to my heart, filling my eyes with ridiculous tears at her praise. "You won," she murmurs. She kisses me gently and turns to go. I know with sudden clarity she won't be back.

"Come tomorrow," I plead. "I'll miss you." It surprises me to realise I will.

She pauses, and shakes her head.

"Who will teach me?" I ask.

"You're truly the Master now," she whispers. Those wonderful, wise eyes reach deep inside me; her smile fills my heart with love. She knows why I lost, and I can say no more as her long, lithe legs take her away.

The sun in the square is never as bright again, after Charlie leaves. In the years that come and go, Old Tony's bench becomes empty one hot summer's day. I take his place, chortling as I watch the fierce competition of the newcomers. Recently retired, they come to the square looking to replace the emptiness.

"You were a Grand Master once, Jeremy," some particularly foolish soul will say. "Don't you want to show me how chess can be played?"

I see in his eyes he thinks he can't lose. So, I haul my creaking bones off the smooth stone bench and play the game. As conceited as I once was, the young warrior thinks his skills give him the victory.

Afterwards, I return to my bench. Old Tony's cackle whispers faintly round the square, although it is I who laugh. As I lean back and raise my face to the sun, Charlie's last smile shines against the inside of my closed eyelids: a dazzling memory of what love is.

Whispers of Love *first appeared in* Notes from Underground: An Anthology, *published by The Literary Lab (USA) in February, 2011.*

In the Shadow of the Moon

At first I almost don't see the flash of grey, scampering across the road. Then it pauses, its nose rising up to the moon. Does it scent the answer it seeks on the chill night breeze? My headlights catch the long ears, the beady eyes staring, unblinking, until the hare vanishes, as quickly as it appeared.

Shaken for the second time this evening, I stop the car.

"Drive on," you say. "What if another car comes?"

"Not on this road," I answer, leaning across you to scrabble in the glove compartment for the half-used pack of Marlboros I discarded last week when I gave up smoking, again. "Nothing comes along here at night."

"We're here," you say, and press back in your seat, afraid that my arm will brush your breasts. Those sacrosanct breasts that are mine no longer.

I look at the crossroads ahead.

To the left, the river.

To the right, the mountains.

And only a desert straight ahead.

Oh, it's not really a desert. It's farmland, lush with corn and potatoes; a few fields left fallow to ensure good crops in the coming years. Without you, it's a desert waiting to suck me dry.

"Let's go," you urge nervously, for I'm always in a hurry.

Tonight, though, I drag slowly on my smoke and stare at the crossroads, seeing the signs but not seeing them as my mind travels back to dinner.

#

"I want a divorce," you blurt over the soup.

It's butternut, my favourite, thick with cream and a dash of nutmeg, sliding smoothly down my throat.

I pretend I don't hear you. "The soup is delicious." I call the waiter across. "Ask the chef if he'll give my wife the recipe." A politely murmured assent and he fades away again.

But your ugly lie stays.

“Did you hear what I said?” you ask. Demand.

“The harvest will be good this year,” I say, between sips of my soup. I savour each taste, carefully, deliberately, dipping into the thickness, feeling how I force the spoon through the liquid resistance with a subtle strength.

You give up and ask about the expected tonnage.

#

We’re not alone in the darkness after all. The hare skitters back. More confident now, it stops in the path of the headlights, ears and whiskers twitching as it lifts its face to the full moon.

I laugh at its antics and you jerk in surprise as the creature scurries away past the sign that says ‘CAUTION: FLASH FLOODS IN SUMMER.’

I laugh again: my decision is made. Tossing the stub out of the window I start the car. It’s not summer any more, so where does the danger lie?

“W-where are we going?” you ask.

“Home,” I say, “by the long road.”

I see you don’t understand, not even when I pass the hare and head straight into the moon.

I leave it far behind as we hit the bridge at full speed, the sound of my laughter drowning out the squeal of tyres slipping and sliding into the darkness where we will rest.

Ragman

At first, she thought someone had lost a coat. Crumpled and discarded under the city bench—half its wooden slats missing, used for firewood one long ago winter—the pile of rags lay unmoving.

Fresh from the country, despite her age on the wrong side of thirty and her appearance of a sophisticated businesswoman, she was naïve. And, as the shadows in her eyes and the faint frown that had taken up permanent residence on her forehead since the day she'd moved to the city testified, perhaps a little frightened.

But she had courage, that one, although she didn't know it then. The city would test her, and test her again, trying to break her innocence. She fought the loss, oh, she fought it hard, without even knowing what she was doing. Her courage and her endurance were so much part of her, she never noticed when she called them forth from her hidden depths.

Today, with that pile of rags, the city tested her for the first time.

The coat moved and she saw it contained a man.

The tramping feet of the city dwellers parted like the Red Sea for Moses around the ragman. Slowly, he pulled himself into a sitting position. His skeletal hands, on stick thin arms, covered with dirt and grime, had hardly enough strength to push.

When he fell back onto one elbow, his swaying head heavy on his scrawny black neck, she could stand it no more. Uncaring of the smart new suit she'd bought for her new job in Penmore Towers in downtown Johannesburg, she rushed to his side.

"Hold on," she said, almost gagging at the smell of booze and shit and months of unwashed sweat. "Let me help you."

"Leave him," a passer-by said. "He's an old drunk."

"He may be ill," she said. The man rushing by never saw the disapproving frown she gave his callousness, because he'd already walked on.

The ragman, boneless from drink or starvation or both, was too heavy. No one else offered help, not even unwanted advice. She couldn't find a policeman. She knew no one. In the end, all she could do was take out some money and tuck it into a torn pocket. Rewarded with a vague grin, revealing a mouth with more gaps than teeth, she said sternly, like a mother to a recalcitrant child, "Use it to buy food. Not drink or *dagga*!"

"*Ja, Nkosikani*," he said, his head bobbing up and down like a yo-yo stretched too far on the arc of its elastic.

Looking at her watch, its brown leather strap and slim gold face the only elegant thing left of her outfit, she clicked her tongue.

"Late on my second day. That's no way to make a good impression!"

It wasn't the way she wanted to start this new life she'd come to claim for herself, either.

"Food!" she reminded the sad bundle of rags at her feet and turned her back on him, running through the revolving doors of the towering grey and black office block.

Pressing the lift button for the 12th floor, she had a clear view of the ragman tottering towards the small liquor store tucked between the Black is Beautiful hairdresser and the grilled-up entrance to the bank. As the lift doors whooshed shut, she sighed and rested her head against the cold steel walls. Her throat tightened and she fought back the tears. The city had won that round.

Crabwalk

There are times in this busy life of mine when I just want to give up the struggle. The constant scuttling hither-and-thither, collecting a crust of bread here, a fallen crumb there, hardly enough to keep body and soul alive.

Every day, the same struggles. Over and over, letting the tides of life wash me up to the beach, frantically clawing my little hole in the sand, all the while avoiding being trampled on by those feet bigger and crueller and more dangerous than mine could ever be.

Even the small ones I must avoid: covered in brightly coloured shells, or bare and pink, those tiny toes belong to shrieking creatures, curious enough to poke sticks down my hole and treacherous enough to almost succeed in murdering me.

That's why I'm missing an eye; one of the nastier young managed to break it off right at the bottom of my eyestalk. I've often wondered how they breed so much. Don't red knots eat their eggs before they hatch?

"Henrietta J. Crab," I said to myself that day, "you're an old fossil and getting older!"

And I am. I feel it in my claws, when they creak and groan as I dig fast to get beneath the safety of the sand.

It's getting harder, too, to fight the current back to my hole in the small, secret rock pool underneath the lighthouse.

Every day it's harder to find the meaning in the struggle.

What's most difficult, though, is fighting the temptation to let go when the next wave, or the next and the next, comes in and sweeps me back into the ocean's deep silence.

One day, perhaps, I'll just sink into that warm rush of water and close my eye without a struggle.

Where There Is Nothing

The moon had set by the time Luthando walked to the meeting stone on the day that she brought water to the village.

With a heavy sigh, she rubbed her back and groaned, for her unborn baby pressed hard against her as she joined the other women. Collecting water was safer when they were together. Danger often lurked along the well-worn path, lined with aloes that bloomed red in the winter. They could never stop to admire them; it took two hours just to reach the water in the neighbouring village of Momgona.

By the time the women came back, the sun was high. Thando had lost half her water. She'd tripped, and her yellow plastic quarter drum had wobbled alarmingly on her head.

"I'm hungry, Thando," her husband called as he saw her. "Get me some food."

A village councillor, he sat with the Chief in the shade of the Great Tree, discussing the day's important matters. Still, she hoped he'd started the fire.

"I'm coming," she said, ducking into the cool dimness of their hut. The sleep mats she'd painstakingly woven last winter were rumpled, and the thatch needed repairs again.

Lifting the water bottle from her head, she placed it carefully on the floor. She arched backwards, her hands kneading her spine before sliding round to rest on her distended belly. She thought of the work waiting: today, tomorrow and all the days of her life.

How would she be able to care for this child? How would she feed it? The sangoma had told her it was a girl. Was this what she wanted for her daughter, this life of drudgery and toil?

If they had water running to the village centre, like the women at Momgona, she could grow vegetables. She would grow more than they ate, and sell them, saving the money. Then this child she carried beneath her heart could have a life better than her mother's.

Luthando heard the murmur of male voices, the bursts of laughter, before her husband called again. "Woman," he said. "Are you sleeping? Bring me the food. Bring enough for the Chief!"

She closed her eyes. Asking her ancestors for strength, she walked back into the sunlight to face the men of the village. Tipping her knee respectfully, she spoke.

"Husband, I am tired of fetching water. This is the New South Africa. You and the Chief must spend our money on pipes to bring water to the village."

They laughed. They ignored her. And, finally, when she didn't move, they got so angry their shouts brought the villagers running.

"Luthando," the women cried, casting anxious glances at the rumbling men. "Our mothers, and our mother's mothers, and their mothers before them, have fetched water. We can do the same."

Hot and tired, Luthando wavered. Then her baby kicked and she knew what she must do. Shrugging off the restraining hands, she walked right up to the Chief.

"My brother," she said, and gave him the look she'd given him when their parents were away in Umthatha, and she had fed and bathed him. "We need water in this village!"

She heard her baby's first cry on the same day the village elders blessed the water from the tap. Luthando strolled out to where everyone danced and sang, praising the gods and the ancestors.

"Look," she whispered to the babe sleeping safely in her arms. "Look at the miracle that will change your life!"

The Leap

I walk and walk. The highway becomes a road and the road becomes a track and the track becomes a rough dirt path. I need to break off a stout stick to help me climb over the pebbles and the occasional boulder.

My breath comes in short thick gasps, drowning out the cry of the small *bokmakierie* sitting high atop a thorny akasia. *Kwit-kwit, ka weeet, ka weeet ... koki, koki, koki* comes the answering duet until, in a green and yellow flash, the pair flies to the safety of a higher tree.

On I walk, on and upwards, leaving the dry grasslands behind until the air gets thinner and the sweat drips from my forehead despite the heavy cool clouds that swirl around the path and obscure my view.

I thought I knew where I was going.

"I'll follow the sun," I'd said, when Papa asked me where I'm headed. The yellow light is still ahead of me, a dull glow above the cloud-covered peaks in the distance.

"When will you be back?" Mama had asked.

"When the sun and the earth are as one," I'd replied. "When man and beast lie side by side."

I left them, shaking their heads at my folly.

Now I am weary, from too many miles and too many wrong turns that have forced me to retrace my steps, no longer eager and adventurous, but dragging through the dust.

I sigh. Here is another choice. I have come to a fork in the road. One has no marking and heads north, into the sun and vast blue sky. The other has a sign I must lean in close to read.

'Backhome' say the faded red letters, and I anchor my weariness on the stick that has helped me get so far.

Home. The word warms me to my very marrow, conjuring up images of fecund women, waiting, waiting as the moon waxes and wanes, as the seasons come and go.

Home: a place of timeless time, where we can gather wild flowers from the banks of the muddy rivers and stroll home across the dry grassland, scattered with pink and white cosmos, their daisy heads dancing in the quiet evening breeze.

Home, the wind whispers as I turn and head for the other path, the one that has no name and no memories.

Soon, too soon, I stand on the rough edge of a cliff. The sharp black granite cuts through my thin sandals and my heart thump-thumps its nervous beat through my blood.

I shuck my coat and toss aside the stick I no longer need. With one deep breath, I leap. There is no going back home now, I think, as the wind rushes past my face and the rough calico of my dress flutters like angel wings behind me.

As I fall and fall through the empty sky, the voices of my past clamour and call, wail and whine, through the rushing air. I let them go. I let them all go as first I tumble and then I soar: soar into the vast silence that is my faith and my surrender.

And there, far below me, where the sun and the earth meet once more, I am transformed. I am home, where the beasts still lie down with man and all is silent and peaceful.

Goldy's Locks

The first time I dye my hair blonde, my husband calls me Goldy. Somehow the name sticks, so that even now, when I look in the mirror and see nothing but thin grey strands that feel somehow alien to me, I'm still called Goldy.

Forty-nine years we were married, forty-nine years, six months, three days, four hours and fifty-eight minutes. A lifetime. Or, at least, the only part of a lifetime that counts.

And it's all over in a second. A short sharp explosion and his heart stops forever at two minutes to five one icy winter morning.

The silly jig of the phone, too cheerful for a day like today, shakes me from my melancholy.

"Hello, Mom." My son's voice, so like that of his father's, echoes at me down the telephone wire.

"Shaun," I say, before he can say what I know he wants to. "Shouldn't you be at work already?"

He says it anyway. "Today would have been your fiftieth wedding anniversary, Ma."

A silence falls over the invisible cord that connects us. A silence heavy with loss, yet bright with memories. Some are good ones, like holding this child of mine, now a man with his own children, for the first time, while Geoff waited outside. Others, the ones that have me sitting alone in my small room, day after day, Shaun knows nothing about.

"I know," I say, when the silence gets too dense. "I'm sorry."

"So am I."

I feel how he hesitates, trying to find a way to ask all the questions he wants to. Eventually, he condenses it into a simple phrase.

"Are you okay?" His voice wobbles at the end, reminding me of too long ago, when that same wobble fought back tears after falling off his bicycle and he didn't want his father to see him cry. Now, as then, my heart aches for the inevitable pain I can't save my son from.

So I lie, to give him peace. "I'm fine, my boy. Nothing to complain about."

"What do you do all day?"

"Read, and knit." I shrug nonchalantly. "I've finished another sweater for you."

We sit in another silence, each wrapped in the heat of our memories, until he bursts out, "If Dad was so bad, why didn't you say anything to me earlier?"

"I didn't know how bad it was until the end." I can see he doesn't understand how I couldn't know. Sometimes I wonder if I should have seen little clues, hints that all was not as it should be, earlier. Could there have been another way, a solution other than the bloody breaking of a heart?

"If only you'd spoken to me," Shaun cries. "Maybe Dad would still be with us."

Anger licks away some of my concern for his pain, as if his father's death makes me see how alike they are. He adds, "Everything would still be the same."

"Everything changes. Your father was old and ill," I say. A gentle bite sharpens the words. Since Geoff's death, I'm unable to suppress my feelings as well as I did for all those years I was married.

Shaun still has me, in a way, but like his father, he takes my presence for granted, until it's too late to change anything.

My son, however, doesn't see this. He's young, and his wife loves him with the illusions of youth and security. I paid too high a price for my security. Nearly fifty years and now, when I should be free, still I'm locked away.

"Goldy," the guard says, "this isn't a scheduled visit. I can't allow you any more time."

Despite the square solidity of her body in the ugly grey-green uniform, she is the most compassionate of the troop guarding the women's prison. Perhaps it's her nature; more likely, my age makes her gentle with me. "Say goodbye to your son."

With one notable exception, I've been obedient all my life, so it's not difficult to touch my hand to the glass that separates me from Shaun. Our fingers touch, yet don't touch.

"Goodbye, Shaun." I smile, and utter a mother's eternal promise. "Don't worry about me; I'll be fine." Only the fact that I can't scoop him up into my arms as I used to when he was a child breaks my control. I forget my earlier irritation, and my sobs are as noisy as his are silent beyond the thick heavy glass separating us. "Give my love to Mandy and the kids."

I put the phone down before I hear the silent plea I see his lips make. "Why?" he cries. "Tell me why?"

How do you tell a son why you killed his father? I have no answer for him. So, I get out of the chair, and walk away, through the door the guard holds open. I'm pleased when I hear the key turn solidly in the lock.

Locks have been part of my life as far back as I can remember. Yet, there's an odd sort of comfort in these locks keeping me confined to my solitary cell. They're real. Hard steel squares that make no pretence at being anything other than what they are: unequivocal restraints keeping me separate from the world I should inhabit.

"Here we are, Mrs Brom." Dolly's mouth, as square as the rest of her, twists in a parody of politeness, as if she's a porter leading me to a luxury hotel room.

"Thank you, Miss Dolly. You're very kind." There's no harm in pandering to her ego, is there? I've had enough practice at getting just the right amount of gratitude in my voice, without the descent into open sycophancy. Forty-nine years, six months, three days, four hours and fifty-eight minutes of practice, to be exact. Oh, sorry—that should be fifty-seven minutes.

It's in the fifty-eighth minute I reach for the gun.

"I've had enough, Geoff," I say. "I'm not taking any more. I'm not getting out of bed." I'd felt the chill of the morning when I'd got up earlier to pee. "Why don't you make your own tea for a change?"

The stillness from his side of the bed we've shared since the beginning of our marriage is so deep I think at first he's fallen asleep again.

Then, "You will make my tea," he says quietly.

"No."

The blankets shift as he sits up, crackling in the cold. "Yes," is all he says, "you will. It's your duty as my wife."

I find it surprisingly easy to open the lock that has bound me to his side for so long. "No," I say again, and pull the trigger.

Like I say to the judge six weeks later, there was no rage, just emptiness. I'd given too much emotion, for too long, for too little in return.

There is only a sense of relief as the noise fades away, leaving me to savour—for the first, and only, time in my life—the joy of being unlocked, of being free.

I wait a while, warm and cosy in my bed. Then I pick up the red-speckled telephone and dial my son.

"Your father's dead," I say, when Shaun mumbles a greeting into the phone.

"Oh my God, Ma!" Grief and shock sweep the last traces of sleep from his voice. "I'll be there as quick as I can."

"Thank you, Shaun." Too calm, and relaxed, I shock him. But not as much as I shock him when I open the door a scant fifteen minutes later.

He stands there, a tall, thin man with his hair just beginning to recede, a solemn-looking priest standing next to him.

"Ma!" is all he can say, *"Ma!"* He enfolds me in a loving embrace. I return it clumsily, the gun beginning to drag my wrist down with its weight.

"I'm glad you're here, son." And I am, although I also wish him a million miles away where he won't have to face the pain awaiting him. "You'd better take this," I say, and hand him the gun. "The police might need it."

He looks blankly at the grey metal. "What's this?"

"A key," I say.

And my laughter, light and unburdened, follows him as he stumbles on the sight of his father's body, already cold in the bitter winter air.

Burnt Offerings

Soft. Fluffy. Ma said if she could catch it, she could hold it.

It hopped here, past her feet. Then it hopped there, under the bush Ma was so proud of, the one with the purple flowers that Ma dried and she crushed, so that Ma could sew them into little cushions to put in her clothes drawers. The sun made her face hot and damp. She ran faster, almost grabbing the bobbing white tail.

When Ma and Pa and Bethy started laughing, she glared back over her shoulder to where Pa stood, his bare chest shining wet, as he leaned over the braai, pushing the flames higher and higher with the fork. Ma was behind him, bringing out the meat for him to cook. Ma put the meat down on the square wire table, the white paint peeling where she'd picked and picked at it.

"Bethany," Ma said to Little Sus, "help your sister catch the rabbit."

She could do this herself. She could! She could! With a sudden lunge she fell on the bunny, panting in the shade of the purple bush. The flowers smelt sweet as she squeezed the bunny tight, tight like the ball of fire burning in her chest, as she walked to where they stood around the braai, laughing and clapping and cooing.

"Here," she said as she reached the fire, blazing high as Pa poked it again. "I don't like it anymore."

She tumbled the bunny into the flames and, as she turned to pick up her doll, she ignored Ma's screams and Pa's curses and the high-pitched squeals of the stupid rabbit that had made her run and run until everyone laughed at her.

#

Bethany never forgot that day. A perfect summer's day: the pale blue sky bleached by the sun; the water in the new pool twinkling and sparkling and, finally, awfully, the smell of burning fur and burning flesh as Pa dropped the braai fork and grabbed her pet rabbit from the consuming flames.

It died before Pa had got the car out. Something else died too. Bethany knew then there would be no happy families for the Karee family. No more pets. No friends to sleep over. No peace.

Just the four of them: Pa, Ma, Bethany and Marie.

Marie, who would never, could never, grow up, but who would control them all until there was nothing left for any of them except her demands and Bethany's dreams.

Piercing the Sky

Nock the arrow.
Breathe in.
Draw.
Breathe out.
Release and, before the arrow flies straight and true into the distant straw target, slide the next one out of the quiver and begin again.

From the first time Andrew lifted the bow, the steady rhythm consumed him.

The twang of the bow vibrating, the heavy thwack as the arrow hits the gold centre, called to something in his soul. A forgotten darkness; a germ of ancient strength buried deep inside. He never knew it existed until, having watched the archery instructor carefully, he picked up the bow, nocked the arrow as smoothly as if he'd done it a thousand times before, steadied his eye, his arm, his breath … and came alive.

That first day he went back home full of excitement. "Mama," he called, when he walked into the kitchen with its lacy white curtains, plastic yellow flowers and small pine table making it his favourite room in the house. He emptied the debris from his lunch box into the garbage disposer and walked over to the sink to rinse it, shaking off the water before placing it on the draining board. Mama didn't like it if he just dumped dirty dishes in the sink.

"More work for me," she'd say, "as if your father didn't leave me with a hard enough life when he died."

Andrew always did his best to make Mama's life easier. He took her coffee every morning and listened as she lay in bed telling him about how badly she'd slept because the bugs had kept her awake all night, and the trees had creaked and moaned, reminding her how sore her legs were and how they ached and ached …

He would place the tray, decorated with her favourite cloth and with the morning paper next to her mug of coffee, across her lap. Then he'd step back as she took her teeth out of the glass on the side table, half filled with pink Sterident, and settle them in her mouth with a loud smack of her lips before picking up the coffee mug.

He'd wait anxiously for her first slurp of the liquid and, as she sighed with pleasure, he'd ask, "Would you like me to rub your legs this morning, Mama?"

She'd rest her palm, still warm from the hot coffee, against his cheek and say, as she did every morning, "That would be lovely!" Then she'd give his cheek a quick double pat and add, "No mother could ever ask for a better son. You're Mama's little prince, aren't you?"

"Always," he'd say as he fetched the Sloane's Heat Rub from the bathroom. He'd carefully fold the blankets back over Mama's knees. Putting an old towel under her legs, he'd squeeze the smelly white cream into his palm, warming it first then, as he'd done from when he was five years old and Pa had died, he'd slowly work the magic cream into Mama's legs, sliding it between her toes and all the way up to where the blankets stopped mid-thigh.

At first he loved watching Mama wiggle her toes. When she sighed with relief, he'd feel strong and useful, like the man in the house. But he never told Mama when, around the time the first fuzz appeared on his chin, it made him feel strange. He came to hate the task, especially the days she'd shaved her legs and her skin was smooth and soft and not like a Mama's skin should be. It did things to him that he knew Mama wouldn't like: he felt an inner stirring, a shifting from prince to warrior.

He remembered that feeling the first time he lifted the bow and, with barely a pause and much to the surprise of his colleagues, shot every arrow dead into the target's centre.

That was the day even the kitchen was different when he arrived home. The hum of the bowstring as he loosed the arrow still rang in his ears as he called again, "Mama! Mama? Where are you?"

"Don't shout," she said from behind him. "How often have I told you boys don't become young gentlemen if they behave like hooligans?" She looked cross and he knew she was missing Pa again.

He wanted to tell her he wasn't a boy any more—he was twenty-six next birthday—but she also looked tired. Her hair, the same red as his, showed some grey streaks and the rubber-soled flats and thick hose she wore hid her legs; those legs that weren't so smooth any more when he rubbed them in the morning, but lumpy with varicose veins. Even her face wasn't as beautiful today. The skin under her eyes was thick and baggy, and the dark red lipstick she wore bled slightly into the small cracks around her turned-down mouth.

"Sorry, Mama," he said and, because he loved her, he clamped down on the energy bubbling inside him since that first arrow had sung its way across the bare grass to find its mark with a satisfying, solid sound.

"What did you want to tell me?" she asked.

"Nothing," he said, shifting uncomfortably as her eyes scanned him from his head to his toes. "I just wanted to say hello."

As he ran his hands down the stiff creases of his smart sta-press trousers—in the Prince of Wales grey check pattern that Mama herself chose because, she said, Pa had looked so good in them way back when they fell in love in the 70s—he thought longingly of blue jeans. Everyone else, including Aisha who shared his booth at the call centre where he worked, wore jeans at the archery class.

Aisha had put his name down for the archery classes when the email first came round. "It'll be fun, Andrew," she'd said, and tossed her straight black hair back over her shoulder with a graceful twist of her hands. A disobedient strand had slid in a silky wave over her—he swallowed as he thought of it—over her bosom and distracted him.

"I'll go," he said, before he was thinking properly. He'd liked the way she'd tapped his cheek and said, "Good boy!" Her black eyes had sparkled, her teeth flashing white against her golden-olive skin, as she laughed. He hadn't thought then what Mama would say.

He never did tell Mama about that first archery class. He lied about the call centre being short-staffed and him working late. And he never told her how, every morning, every lunch hour, and for two hours every night after work, he went to the archery field.

"You're a natural, Andrew, are you sure you've never practised archery before?" the instructor said, as Andrew braced the lower limb of the bow against his foot, pulling and pushing it as easily as a twig as he slid the string towards the notches. "If you keep it up, you'll win the championship."

How could he tell the man it had nothing to do with winning, but everything to do with a mysterious longing? When he addressed the target, when he slowly drew in his breath, his arm strong and steady, he was no longer Andrew, Valerie Skinner's dull, quiet boy: he was once again a Prince of Scythia.

And, as he looked along the shaft of the arrow, every sound disappeared; every bird and every blade of grass faded away, until all he could see and all he could hear was the memory of a long-forgotten plain in an ancient land. Once he was a warrior, standing tall amongst his people, the flaps of his soft conical cap, with its intricate embroidery matching the wide collar on his belted tunic, brushing against his beard shining red in the cold winter sun.

That strength, long buried in the mists of his soul until first he touched the bow, would leak into his body as he stood, Pa's trousers with their sharp creases flapping against his legs, because Mama refused to buy him jeans. "Gentlemen," she said, "do not wear denim."

As a hum grew in his chest, he would take a long, slow breath in, unleashing that power from the recesses of his being until his anxieties and his fears and his Mama were nothing but a wraith vanishing in the wind. He stood, bow in hand, shooting arrow after arrow after arrow, and flowed with the wind, aiming at the target. Then he'd breathe out, and release a little part of himself too, a joyous cry drowned by the victorious cheers of a long-dead army.

Even when he was alone, the early morning dew making his sturdy leather shoes slip on the grass, he would live for those whimsical cheers. They drew him back, day after day, month after month, whatever the weather. Nothing could stop him; not even Mama's suspicions when she asked him why his pay was so much less when he was working so many extra hours. He'd told her of the bow and arrows he'd bought, and why. Her tears hurt him, but the imperative to pierce the sky with his arrows was so urgent, so all-consuming, he could not, would not stop.

Later he even bought himself a pair of boots that gripped the ground as he stood, legs wide apart, alive again to the sound of a horse dying next to him as he regained his balance and, lifting the heavy bow, he sunk into the silence, that great silence where only the wind called his name and he heard nothing until his troops rallied round him crying … *Andras … Andras, the enemy king is dead. Great is your victory, O Prince Andras!*

Andrew blinked his eyes and slowly lowered the bow, until the point rested on the tip of his boot. He shaded his eyes with his hand and gazed towards the distant target face, its brightly coloured circles marred only by the unyielding arrow quivering in the centre. He turned to look for the voices that cheered him on, but there was no one, not even Mama, and so he lifted the bow again and again until his arm ached and the sweat poured down his face and he could no longer hear them calling him prince.

He spent so much time at archery classes, Mama no longer called him prince either. As he walked the distance to collect his arrows, packing them and his bow neatly away, he told himself he must remember to tell Mama he would not be home for dinner tomorrow night. After the archery lessons were over, Aisha would take him to buy a pair of jeans. "Blue jeans," she said, looking him over in a way that reminded him of Mama at times, "to match your blue eyes." Then she'd tossed her hair in the way that made her breasts roll softly and his mouth suddenly dry out.

Mama was in bed when he arrived home. "Andrew, is that you?" Her querulous voice drifted down the stairs.

"Yes, Mama," he called, and dumped his dirty lunch box in the sink.

He'd wash it later, he decided. Then he bent to take a jar of wax from the cupboard beneath the old sink and, with long careful strokes perfected from years of rubbing magic cream on Mama's legs, he started to spread the wax over the slenderness of his bow.

A Butterfly Kiss

The grave is small, smaller than she expected. “It should be deep to hold such a big heart,” she thinks as she stares unseeingly into its depths, “and to bury so much love.”

She is dry-eyed, her loss unable to find expression beyond the endless, polite thank-yous she murmurs to the mourners who crowd her with awkward hugs and mumble clichés about knowing how she feels and being sorry for her loss.

“You’re too young to be a widow,” they add and shake their heads. “Sad, so sad, he was in the prime of his life,” they say for lack of any other words, and pat her arm with a clumsy sympathy that cannot fill the wide emptiness within her.

A whisper passes her ear; the brave red ribbon looped around the hat she wears to protect her from the summer heat has attracted a lone butterfly. Her hand drifts up to brush it away. It won’t leave. With a stubborn flap, it alights on the brim of her hat; on her shoulder; her arm; anywhere it can touch her. Then, in its own time, it meanders away to kiss the flowers resting on top of the coffin.

There it stays, until the first thump of soil lands in the grave and chases it away. As it leaves, she hears her beloved’s whisper again.

Watching the butterfly float upward, her tears begin to fall, the first tear for sadness and the second for joy.

Where Heartaches Don't Show

"A tenner at 12 o'clock," Vern said, and let the smoke slide sideways out his pursed lips, his left eye squinting shut against the wispy coil.

Pete gripped his whisky tumbler tighter. He heard Vern, but he was listening to the echo of Elaine's threats as he'd slammed out the house this morning. Sometimes he wished they'd both grow up. But Elaine knew he loved her too much and Vern, with his charming blue eyes and his pretty face, had always found life—and women—too easy.

"Quick!" Vern kicked his barstool. "You're going to miss her!" He wasn't going to stop until Pete looked.

Pete jabbed his thick horn-rimmed spectacles back up his nose with one finger, his eyes never leaving the amber liquid lapping at the edges of the glass. There was a chip in the rim. Tiny cracks radiated outward from that broken centre. Like the cracks in a broken heart, Pete thought, and his mouth wobbled alarmingly as he remembered Elaine's face as she shouted that she'd leave him, leave him, if he didn't make life more exciting for her.

Didn't she know after all these years that he couldn't do exciting? It was always Vern who was off climbing Kilimanjaro or kayaking around Madagascar. Pete, well, Pete stayed in his office working all hours and never asked Vern to pay back the money he borrowed to live that exciting life Elaine so envied when he told her about Vern's latest adventure.

Sighing, he looked up at Vern's next jab. "Where is this looker?" he asked and swung the barstool in the direction of Vern's nod so fast that his skinny ass almost slid off the shiny red imitation leather. The chair squeaked as he settled himself more comfortably and let his gaze drift through the stale cloudy air.

"Mmm-hmmm-mmm!" Vern murmured and made smacking noises with his lips. "If the rest of her is as fuckable as her legs, I won't be lonely tonight."

Vern was right, as he usually was about women. The woman was a beauty. Mahogany hair rippled over her shoulders. Her legs started at ankles, trim above high black stilettos, and stretched all the way up to a tiny strip of silver spandex that some would call a skirt.

There was something achingly familiar about the shape of those legs, Pete thought. They reminded him of how Elaine had looked on their honeymoon. Standing on the beach in Mauritius in a tiny bikini, her legs had also stretched to infinity and she'd tossed her hair back over her shoulder just like this woman tossed …

"Christ!" he yelled, and swiped Vern's elbow off the bar so that Vern's head jerked and bounced and his lascivious gaze lost its target. "Get your eyeballs back in your face, you dirty bastard!"

"Ow!" Vern complained, as he rubbed his chin. "Why you do that? I almost dislocated my jaw!"

"That's Elaine!"

"Elaine?"

"My wife!"

Vern looked as confused as he felt. "The looker with the legs is Elaine?"

He nodded and his heart thumped as he saw the same challenge slither into Vern's eyes that always gleamed there when Vern saw something he knew he shouldn't have. "I forgot I said she must meet me here for a drink," Pete lied. "She wants to meet my work buddies."

Vern laughed as he slid off his stool and squashed his cigarette in the nearest ashtray.

"Well, then, my forgetful friend," he said. "Let's go and join your pretty wife."

Pete watched as, with the ease he'd always envied him, Vern strolled over and touched Elaine on the shoulder.

She smiled up at him, even as Pete managed to unclench his fists and order her favourite drink.

The Fishermen

The crash of the waves on the rocky outcrops first woke him. He lay in the semi-darkness, listening to the tent flap overhead, almost drowning the sound of Jamie's snores.

Was he dreaming, or had his son grown in the two weeks since he'd last seen him?

Jack lifted a hand out from his sleeping bag and stretched his naked arm to rest it on the small arm flung restlessly over the edge of the camp bed. Even in sleep, Jamie's fists clenched and unclenched with worry.

Jack sighed. Their weekend together was almost over. He'd have to tell him today, he thought as he lay back.

Through the splitting seam of their old tent, he watched the sky turn pale and pink as the wind died to a breeze and listened as the waves calmed.

With the decision made, he threw back the unzipped sleeping bag and stood up. Better to get this day over.

Angie was still unforgiving. He'd wondered what excuse she'd use this time to prevent him taking Jamie away for the father-time so carefully allotted by the court. If Angie had had her way, he'd never see Jamie. Thank God Greg was a good lawyer. The best.

And the best of men, as well.

"Come on, Jamie," he said. "Time to catch our breakfast."

His heart clenched with love as those soft blue eyes, so like his own, flickered open and that easy-going smile came and went, too quickly replaced by the uncertainty that resided there ever since Angie had confronted him and he'd moved to Greg's place.

Later, as he and his son stood at the edge of the sea and the easy, rhythmic spin of the reels lulled him, he broached the subject.

"Did Mom tell you my news?" he asked casually.

Jamie's face clenched with hope, before becoming carefully impassive. He was too young to have learned to hide his hopes and his pain, and Jack hated that he'd soon add a bigger burden to those slender shoulders.

Jamie shook his head cautiously. "What news, Dad?"

His son still dreamed of the happy family he'd once thought they were: Jack, Angie and Jamie. He'd thrown enough hints on the rare occasions his parents where in the same room.

Jack hesitated, and lost courage. "You know I love you," he said, instead of what he should say. "I'll always love you, just as Mom will always love you."

Fishing was forgotten, even though the bob of the line showed more than seaweed had caught on the lure, and Jamie swung towards him. "Are you and Mom …?"

"I'm getting married again," he said, as gently as he could, for he knew the words would shatter his son's hopes.

"To Mom?"

He shook his head. "To someone else."

Jamie's bottom lip trembled and he lifted a hand to cover it. "Do I know who you're marrying?"

"Yes," he said, and dreaded the next question.

"Does Uncle Greg know who you're marrying?"

Relief rushed through Jack. Perhaps this wouldn't be as bad as he thought. "Very well," he said, and his hands shook so much he reeled in his line and bent to fiddle with the tackle.

After all the time he'd spent at Greg's house, Jamie liked Greg. "I suppose I'll like her too, then." He twisted that quivering lip and added, "I wish …"

"I know," Jack said. "But Mom and I don't love each other any more. We both love you," he added, "but not each other. We just can't stay married any longer. I'm sorry."

The boy sighed, and shrugged. "That's okay," he said, although Jack knew it wasn't really. Then Jamie noticed the bouncing line and turned back to his fishing.

Jack stopped toying with the smelly old bait and watched as, with the calm acceptance of a child who no longer believes in dreams, Jamie focused completely on his fishing.

He thought about saying more. About telling Jamie all there was still to tell. But he wasn't ready yet.

He was afraid that he'd see in Jamie's eyes the same disgust he'd seen in Angie's eyes, and so he said nothing.

There would be time enough to tell Jamie the rest.

For now, he'll just lean back against the barnacle-sharp rocks and listen to the rush of the waves, the cry of the gulls and the soft whirr-whirr of his son casting his line up and down, up and down, through the salty sea air until it lands in the water and sinks like a stone.

Flash Fiction II

The Old Theatre

silence falls. lights dim.
yesteryear's grand splendour fades
on an empty stage.

In Full Bloom

in the dew-dropped
heart of a red red rose lies
the face of my dream.

High Life

colours of fashions
on cold lifeless bodies hang
in soft folds of spring.

A Distant Dream

A yearning lies within
For all beyond my here-and-now.
Past bare branches,
There in the distance,
The rich glow of life burns seductively.
I can almost touch it, feel it, smell it,
But my vision is blurred
By glass, and rain as wet as tears.
I remain outside, an observer.

The Wheel Turns

I'm suffocating in candyfloss frills.

I must be dreaming, so I lie still, waiting for the dream to end. Then the voice calls to me again.

"Wake up, Daniel," she says. "It is time."

When I try to move, I'm bound to the bed. The irons chafe my wrists and ankles. Yet I feel no pain ... only safety, for what risks lie beyond my chains?

She bends down, blonde hair trailing across my belly, until my groin clenches in unwilling desire. I do not want to feel anything for this woman who is both my captor and my dream.

"I'll set you free." The clink as she unwinds the chains is loud as she adds, "For a short while."

"What did I do wrong? Why am I a prisoner?"

Her reply is gentle. "It's for your own good," she says.

Astounded at the certainty in her voice, I stagger, cursing myself for my weakness, too dull and too tired to think of an easy reply. One that won't anger her, for I don't want the manacles clamped back around my limbs. The shock of my freedom, however illusionary, is too sweet to risk.

"Don't loiter," she says, sounding like my long-dead mother. "We don't have much time."

I follow her outside the small room, my eyes blinking rapidly as they adjust to the scorching sun. The heat sucks me dry. I fling up a hand to stop the blinding glint bouncing off the domed huts scattered before us. She points to the largest dome, tugging my hand.

"Hurry," she urges, "they'll be starting the movie soon."

The mud huts, so finely crafted their walls mirror my shaggy reflection, tower up from the stark, bare landscape. I need a shave, I decide, and the familiar rasp of my hand over my beard gives me an obscure comfort.

"What is that place?" I ask with renewed confidence.

"Tomorrow," she replies, "or yesterday. You decide." She strides off without looking to see if I'm following. The thud of her boots in the dust wakes a dead stick into a snake, which slithers sideways to the safety of a nearby boulder.

We pass the closest hut and an animal scream snaps my gaze towards the barred window. She carries on walking, not even flinching.

Feeling like Eve about to taste her apple, I stop and peer into the darkness. A naked man, thin and bony, lies shivering on the floor, until the uniformed woman holding his leash tugs him to his knees.

"What's she doing?" I call to the woman ahead of me. I cannot ask if the same future awaits me. "She's hurting him!" I add, daring to grasp her arm to draw her to a halt. "Aren't you going to stop her?"

"What must I do?" She shrugs. "She owns him."

"But ... what's he done?"

"He is The Enemy."

"He must have done something," I insist, "to become her enemy."

She thinks a while, a faint crease marring the delicate beauty of her face. "He's different," she finally says. "He is all that we are not."

"Can't you see she's destroying him?" I point to the tears of humiliation rolling down the man's face, as the woman grabs his balls and gives them a lascivious squeeze, a look of bovine pleasure in the flush dulling her cheeks. "How can a woman be so cruel?"

"What are you saying, Daniel? That you've never been cruel to a woman?" She looks at me sceptically. "You've never *accidentally*," she stresses the word harshly, "destroyed a woman?"

Buried memories bring the bile of guilt to my throat. "That's different," I mumble. "I've never physically hurt a woman like she's hurting him."

"What's different about anything you've done?" The hardness in her voice makes me wonder how I'd ever thought her beautiful.

"I'm just a man." I shrug. "I'm human." I laugh weakly, hoping to placate her. "Women should know better."

The blonde stares at me stonily. "You're saying a woman can't be sexually aggressive?"

"N-no!" I stumble over the word in my haste to assure her I'm a 21st century man. Whatever the hell that entails. "All I'm saying is ..."

"Is what, Daniel?" she asks, sounding even more like my mother when I'd done something unforgivably boyish.

"What she's doing ... it's ... it's ..." I pause as fear loosely clutches my bowels. She can do with me what she wants, for I am weak in my vulnerability. I breathe deeply, gathering the dregs of my courage to say, "It's a betrayal of all that's best in a woman's soul."

"Why, Daniel!" She laughs delightedly. "You still think a woman can't commit evil? Dear boy, whatever gave you that idea?"

Her laughter clogs my throat. How can I tell her about the images flaring in my memory? The visions of lullaby hands and soft smiles; the loving sacrifices women have made for millennia.

What would this female—so sure of her power, so confident of her strength—know about such redeeming love? I turn away from her mocking eyes, holding back the words I want to say. The man on the leash howls again, and my grimace is futile.

"We're still learning about our power. Some of us make the wrong choices." Her voice lunges in mild attack. "Like you did."

The accusation in her voice riles me. "I've never treated any woman with such cruelty. Men have kindness in their souls too, just as women can be powerful."

Some vague notions of ancient struggles endured by women confuse me, so I add, "Although some might have made mistakes in using their strength."

"Mistakes?" Her lip curls, showing even white teeth. "Power has many faces, Daniel, and we learnt ours from *you*."

I don't reply, nervous of the anger in her words. She jerks her head towards the large dome, saying, "Come. We've wasted enough time here."

She hustles me along. I barely notice the cold steel walls and woven grass chairs of the hall before the lights dim. The large screen flickers into life, and I sigh comfortably, glad to put the ugliness behind me. My relief doesn't last long.

"That's my brother!" I'm filled with hopeless longing as the camera zooms in on our youthful faces. He's laughing wildly, with the reckless abandon I always admire. His face is so vital, so full of power, I hardly notice the young woman in his arms.

"Look, Daniel, and learn from me," he shouts, before bending his head, grinding his mouth on hers. She whimpers a soft "No!"

She's no match for his strength. Soon she's naked, looking unlike the gentle girl we'd played with all our lives.

My mouth is as dry with excitement now as it was then. Once again, I watch my brother easily push her onto the grass, driving his rigid prick into her bruised and tender flesh, the crescendo of her sobs drowned by his heaving grunts.

I remember the day well.

"Fuck her again, Johnny," my other self urges and my long-ago laughter trumpets mockingly through the hall as I watch my celluloid self stand and do nothing.

My eyes close as a chill whisper touches my neck. I shiver convulsively. In the merciless heat of this land, where does the breeze come from? There are no open doors in the auditorium.

"The movie is a lie," I mutter, to no one in particular.

"It's the truth you were blind to," my mistress reprimands, "when your kind ruled the world."

I glance back at the flashes on the screen before me. For the first time I see the helpless plea in the naked girl's eyes. She stares at me over my brother's bulky shoulder and I see her hopelessness as she flutters weakly, trapped in the cage of our combined force, my brother's muscles and my hurrahs.

I've seen that look before, scouring the face of the man on the leash.

The sob tearing out my throat is uncontrollable. At first, my pain is for my lost illusions; for the girl's secret sorrows and lost dreams. Or perhaps I cry for the crawling man I saw earlier, and for the creature snaring him with her power.

Ultimately I mourn the loss of something far greater than any of us petty creatures.

My tears are for all of humankind, for a simple truth pierces the fog of my ignorance: the wheel turns inexorably.

Only the mask of power changes: it matters not who wields it, for its insidious poison relentlessly corrupts all promises, all hope.

I weep in despair, for who will have the wisdom to see, buried deep within The Enemy, lies the other side of me? Will I have the courage to surrender my quest for power over anything but my own soul and so become immortal?

Searching my filthy clothes for something to wipe my snotty nose, there is nothing but bare skin beneath my rags. I'm about to drag the back of my hand across my face when the stranger behind me reaches over my shoulder, offering a clean white tissue.

Her simple charity undoes me. I turn, collapsing against her breast, until the last of the sobs racking my throat have dried up.

"It's all right, Daniel," she soothes. "We, too, are afraid." After the harshness of my mistress, the husky comfort is a welcome relief.

I must see her face. Such kindness can only belong to an angel. I lift my head, prising open my swollen eyelids to see a face so familiar I think I'm in love. It takes a moment to remember where I've seen those placid features before.

I first saw her a short while ago, dressed in army green and tugging on a man's leash. She is not evil to me now for, this close to her velvet-brown eyes, I can see the anguish driving her.

If I do not hold power over The Enemy, she thinks, *he'll hold it over me. Then I'll be weak once again, and thus will I end.*

Gently I reach up a hand and stroke her cheek. "Free him," I say, "and you will free yourself."

A flash of confusion sparks life into her cow-like eyes, instantly swept away by fear. I see the blow coming long before she wants to hit me.

Proudly I lift my face, for I know what she does not. The only power I have left is that of forgiveness. It is the only power I need and I wield it with all the force I have at my disposal.

"I forgive you," I murmur as the eternal darkness welcomes me. "I love you ... Friend."

A Soldier's Girl

Elsie paused in the process of buttoning her uniform to rub her back. As she waited for the ache to fade into a dull throb, she listened to the incessant plop-plop-plop. The drip from the tap over the old enamel basin, squeezed into the corner of this room with its torn wallpaper, the once-bright roses dulled to a sickly yellow and covered with the mould of decades, drove her crazy.

At home, Father would have called the plumber immediately. Swallowing hard—the upstairs neighbour was cooking tripe and the nausea clawed with bitter acid at her throat—she slid her hands from her back to her swollen belly.

She didn't care what Father said. This was no sin. This small life growing in her was love, real love. Not love that wouldn't stand by a daughter who had said farewell to her soldier in the only way she could.

Catching sight of her reflection in the mirror, Elsie wondered what Gabe would think of her now. The dirty flecks and the grime dulling the mirror's surface didn't hide the rings under her eyes or the lank blonde strands brushing her cheeks. The night before he left, Gabe had buried his face in its soft shiny waves as he'd cried out his love.

Grimacing, she pulled her hair back, twisting it into a tight knot that she held in place with the cheap rubber band she'd filched from the till at Chick-a-Lick when Rathway wasn't looking. It was only a greasy fast-food joint, but he took his duties as manager seriously.

"Thou shalt not steal," he'd say, as grave as Father often was. "A rubber band now; a box of chicken next."

He'd be right. She was starving. This one-roomed dump was smaller than her bathroom at home … no, not home, she reminded herself, at her parent's house, nestled in the leafy cul-de-sac she hadn't seen for months. But it was all she could afford. What with the meagre savings she was putting aside for the baby and the cost of her uniforms … she was sinking fast.

Trying to get a grip on the panic that washed through her, she closed her eyes. The image of the cracked linoleum and the dull lamp with its scorched skew shade burned into her memory. Desperation snapped her into focus.

Picking up the cheap black bag—R10 at Checkers on the sale—she straightened her shoulders. She was a soldier's girl, she told herself sternly, and Gabe would be home soon. He'd marry her and they'd be happy, just the three of them.

She glanced at the buff envelope, with its official-looking stamp. She'd found it pushed under her door when she returned from the night shift late last night. Gabe had said he'd write and let her know when he was coming home. But it wasn't his writing on the envelope.

Looking at the cold, typed letters, she'd decided she was too tired to open it straight away. She'd left it on the green Formica table before engaging in the usual nightly battle with the creaky old sleeper couch. Time enough in the morning to open it before work. Then she'd know how long she still had to wait for her soldier's return.

Flash Fiction III

The Path Less Travelled

Five fluffy faces
Together in formation.
But one swims alone.

A distant shore calls my name,
Alone I swim, but never lonely.
Soft waves slap against the hull
And lull me so I forget:
I seek to escape
Only that which I carry within.

The Cheetah

Run, wild cat, run! run! run!
As fast as you can.
You still can't outrun
Man's greed.

Cry, wild cat, cry! cry! cry!
Soon you will not exist.
Tears mark your lovely face
Man does not care.

The Leopard and the Lizard

In the manner peculiar to the African bushveld, the blood-orange sun sinks quickly, dropping below the solitary line of akasia trees standing sentinel on the horizon.

Still the two men don't move. Not even when the cry of the first jackal sends blistering fingers down their spines, curling fear and anticipation into their bellies. They've waited many years for this night. Years that have passed too quickly—and too slowly.

A small herd of impala grazing at the edge of the camp look at them from careful eyes as the setting sun brushes the last warmth from the day. The black-haired man stands up abruptly, an unwilling smile finding its way to his face as the impala skitter gracefully away, seeking the safety of the dense bush beyond their view.

"Are you ready?" he asks. Almost without waiting for his grey-haired brother's nod, he picks up the drum, easily letting the heavy throb dance through his fingers in concert with the flickering fire at his feet.

"Stop now," his twin says. "You'll scare them away. We must wait."

He nods and, regretfully, puts the instrument aside. They sit in silence, the fire dimming, their thoughts locked inside as they wait for the Great Watcher and her companion to arrive.

Time stretches and pulls, the very air around them twanging with the hum of hidden dreams and broken promises. Black John says bitterly, "They lied."

"They'll be here," Grey John reassures softly, as was his wont. "Don't give up hope."

"I have no hope," Black John sneers. "Hope is for fools."

"You don't mean that."

"I do." Black John shifts sullenly, hunching a shoulder against the rustling air. His brother is a fool and, as he'd promised years—or was it aeons?—ago, tonight will show Grey John what a fool he is. "We should have killed them then." He pauses, the fire reflecting the calculating gleam in his eyes. "Perhaps we still will. Leopard pelts are in demand these days." His fingers scrabble lazily in the dirt finding, and then sensuously smoothing, a small round pebble. "The lizard is too small. It's useless."

"Salamander."

"What?"

"It's a salamander," Grey John says patiently.

"Whatever." With a sharp snap of his wrist, Black John spins the pebble into the glowing embers, enjoying the feel of his muscles rippling and the satisfying hiss as another log collapses under the assault. "There's no money to be made from it. It's too small to make a difference."

"A single thread can make a difference to the cloth it holds together."

"You're wrong."

"We'll see." Grey John finally stands up. There is no difference between the two men, save for the colour of their hair and a gentleness about the eyes Black John lost long ago.

Arching his arms back over his head to ease the ache of waiting, Grey John turns in a slow circle.

"We are born one," he says, "and we will die as one. Why have you fought it for so long?"

"The only thing I've fought is my way to the top."

"She gave you the victory she promised."

"The leopard gave me nothing. Whatever I got I worked for." Black John pushes himself to his feet, his chin aggressively angled towards his brother. "It's *my* success—not hers."

"It's yours, alright," Grey John murmurs wryly. "But is it success?"

"What do you know about success? No one listens to your songs. No one even sings them. Yet, you continue to *hope* that they will. That's not success! Do you want to know what success really is?" his brother demands. "I can do *that*," he snaps his fingers, the click loud in the silence of the starlit night, "and a hundred people will jump to obey me." He strides to the dying fire, kicking it to life again. "Don't tell me it's not success when you have nothing compared with me."

"I have hope."

"Fools have hope. It's all they've got."

"It is enough."

"For you, maybe."

"For you too, if you'd let it."

Black John has had enough. "This is ridiculous. We've waited forever, there's nothing for us here. It was just a stupid kid's dream. A fantasy."

"Why are you so afraid?" Grey John knows why. Watching a nightjar rise from the undergrowth with puffed feathers and an agitated trill, he wonders if his brother knows.

"I'm not afraid. I'm bored."

"Not for much longer." He dusts a hand across Black John's shoulder, nodding towards the path the little bird has flown from. "They come," he whispers and, despite his knowing, he feels the lick of anxiety burst into a flame of fear. Will tonight show Black John the way? Or is he lost until another age?

Then all thought is washed from his mind as the cicadas fall still, the air hovering tautly as they wait.

Into this dense silence the Great Watcher comes, paws puffing up plumes of dust in an even greater silence. The rosettes on her pelt are dark and perfect, a hundred and more eyes, staring in every direction, seeking, watching, carefully cataloguing every tiny corruption in the hearts of men who promise friendship and deliver only lies.

It's her cold liquid eyes, though, which draw the twins closer together as she pads with easy grace towards them. Dark yellow shards look contemptuously at Black John until he stutters accusingly, "You're l-late."

Settling herself in the centre of their makeshift *boma* with all the feline grace inherent in her species, she slowly, with delicate roughness, rasps her tongue over her pelt. She sees how Black John's eyes greedily scan the perfection of her skin.

"Where's the lizard?" he asks. She ignores him and, with a lazy suddenness, unsheathes her claws, apparently intent only on capturing the last hidden burr knotting her fur and marring her beauty.

It annoys Black John, as she'd known it would.

"We've waited forever for you to come." He slants his fists into the pockets of his trousers and, in his foolish arrogance, takes a step closer. "When is the lizard arriving so we can begin?"

"Salamander," the other one says quietly, drawing her suddenly wary eyes towards him. "How many times must I tell you that?"

The grey-haired, silent one makes her nervous. He makes her question her dark power—she's not used to that. As he swivels his head to look at her directly, she knows tonight will test her to the full.

"Greetings, O Great One," the quiet man says. "I've looked forward to this night."

A shiver slides through her body. She stops playing, determined to show him the full force of her strength. Then he will worship her. Then he will fear her, and desire her, as his brother —a man too eager to taste all this life has to offer—does.

Lifting her lips back from the teeth that could easily tear his throat out, she lets the growl echo out of her jaws, proclaiming her greatness to both those who can hear, and those who choose not to hear, the danger hidden in its seductive promise. The ground beneath her paws trembles, and she is pleased.

Black John pales, stepping closer to the fire, wiping his palms down the sides of his trousers.

As if that will save him, she smiles secretly, *when the time comes for him to pay me.*

"That was ... impressive," Grey John says.

She grumbles a snarl at him, not trusting the mildness in his voice. Over the years, she's placed temptation after temptation before him and always he has that same look of resolute meekness about him. The one that makes her wonder where he gets the strength to withstand her, and all that she offers him. It's the lizard's fault.

As if her thoughts conjure the creature up, it scampers into the clearing. So ugly compared with her. So little, she can crush it with one paw.

"You're late, Lizard." She hates that she sounds as petulant as Black John.

"Salamander," Grey John corrects, and starts towards her.

She half rises, the multitude of black eyes rippling into watchfulness over her muscled haunches, bunched now in readiness to strike any threat Grey John offers. He passes her by, and she sinks uneasily back into the dirt.

Gently picking up the cold, small body of the reptile, he says, "I'm glad you came."

The salamander scrambles up his arm to lie panting on his shoulder, looking down at her with eyes that have endured much. Its tail cupping Grey John's neck like a lover's sweet hand unwilling to let go, the creature says, "It's time. Who shall begin?"

The leopard stands up arrogantly. "It is my right."

"Says who?" Black John objects.

"Be quiet," she says, staring at him with casual cruelty in her eyes. "Tonight you finally belong to me." His gaze falls first. "Sit," she orders, and Black John drops like a ripe marula berry to the ground.

"Many cycles of the moon have passed," she begins, once Black John stops wriggling his legs to find a comfortable position, "since we four last met. You were both black-haired boys, identical in nature and in form. Each of you, so full of pride, felt the fire of longing within." Her whiskers twitch; anyone who doesn't know her could think she's smiling fondly.

"It amused me," she continues, "to see you so sure of your purpose. So certain of what you would do and of what you would not do in your noble pursuits. You were both so young then."

Her words whisper the memory, drawing the others in with her until, once again, they stand poised on the edge of a doorway into time ...

#

"Psst! John, do you see that?"

"What? Where?"

"Over there, above the rock in the sun the lizard is lying on."

"Do you see it?" His fingers fumble a bit in his eagerness, for he's never shot a leopard before. He'll earn a fortune if he can kill it cleanly. He recognises the moment the other boy sees it, because he freezes, reverence replacing the sweaty fatigue on his face.

"That ... that's the most beautiful animal I've ever seen," his twin chokes, fear and longing vying for supremacy in his voice. "Don't kill it!"

"Are you mad?" he whispers back. "Of course I'm going to kill it! I want its skin—it'll pay the cost of the bike I've been saving for." As he speaks, he lifts his weapon to his shoulder, fear and nerves forgotten as greed hooks into his heart.

He also forgets that, here, in the busy stillness of the bushveld, the cocking of his weapon is an alien sound. Before he has time to sight the barrel, a mighty roar, like nothing he's ever heard before, rents the air. In a frenzied instant he could never afterwards recall, the leopard stands over him, her fetid breath clogging his nostrils, her great paws keeping him sprawling helpless in the dirt.

"Did you think to destroy me?" the leopard mocks. "*You*, of all puny creatures?" The heat of her scorches his skin, until slowly, slowly, a chill seeps through his frigid body, quenching the torment in his soul.

Then his brother says, "*I* will kill you, if you don't let him go." The sound of metal scraping on metal makes the leopard swivel her head towards him where he stands to their left. She looks at him carefully, measuring the coolness in his eyes and the steadiness of his hand, and she knows he'll shoot her before she can reach him.

"Put the gun down," she purrs, "and I'll give you anything you want."

He looks at her in silence, his finger tightening on the trigger.

"Anything," she whispers, and sees a flicker of temptation bite as the barrel of his gun dips minutely.

"How?" the boy asks. "You're just an animal."

"Are men not animals too? I know your secrets and I have the power you seek."

"Don't trust her," a thin whistle from somewhere over to their right warns. "She'll still get you in the end."

As the reptile speaks for the first time, a flash of anger tarnishes the dull yellow of the leopard's eyes.

"What does such an ugly little creature know?" she asks, not wanting to lose her hold on him. "You will live in opulence and power; you can have it all. Money. Wealth. Control. All that they can buy. Just put the gun down."

The boy looks at the leopard, her ivory teeth scoring scarlet pinpricks across the skin at his brother's throat. He sees the strength in her shoulders; the beauty of her pelt and the power in her paws. He knows he doesn't want to kill her.

Then he looks at the reptile; at its cold, shiny skin; its scrawny legs and even scrawnier tail, and he wonders what use such a tiny creature could have in this world.

"What about my brother?"

"He gets nothing. You get it all." She sees the hunger rise in him, and dips her head so he won't see the triumph in her eyes. "Do you want it?"

"Don't listen to her!" the foolish boy under her paws cries. She stops his protest with a quasi-gentle bite, turning the pinpricks into rivulets of red pooling stickily in the brown dust beneath his neck.

He groans, and lies still. His twin shifts his feet restlessly, the gun in his arms getting heavier. He doesn't know what to do.

"Lizard, will the leopard kill me if I put the gun down?" he asks.

"I'm not a lizard. I'm a salamander."

"Whatever." He shrugs, his soul already dreaming of the riches the leopard promises.

"Refuse the leopard. I will give you something better."

"What can be better than being successful and rich and having everything I want for all of my life?"

"You decide." The salamander slithers awkwardly down the rock, and stands next to the leopard. "Look at me," he says modestly. "I am small, and weak, compared with the leopard and all she can offer. But I can give you what she can't."

"What is that?"

"Hope," the salamander says. "I can give you hope."

"Hope?" The black-haired boy, still as entranced with the leopard's beauty as at the first moment his brother pointed her out, is disgusted. "What use is that?"

"In dark days to come, hope can be your torch."

"Listen to the salamander!" the trapped boy begs.

He has seen into the leopard's dark heart. When she so casually—so easily—tears the skin at his throat, he knows with absolute certainty, that if his brother chooses unwisely, her provocative promise will doom them both. In that instant, every hair on his head turns cold stone grey, the colour of the salamander waiting so patiently for an answer.

The leopard sees the boy waver, the gun barrel beginning to lift again. "Let your brother take the lizard's gift," she offers generously. "You can have my gift, if you promise to come back here when the star of love kisses the moon once again. Then we will decide who has best served their purpose."

"What happens to the one who can find no purpose?" the salamander chimes in.

"I'll eat him, of course." Her head tilts with an inner amusement, and the leopard stands back, freeing the boy she'd captured. She lies down with elegant ease, majestically folding one foreleg over the other, watching him cough and clutch his throat still bearing the marks of her teeth. "Then, for all eternity and beyond, he will be mine." Looking at the boy with the gun, she says. "Make the promise."

"I promise," Black John agrees, knowing with the leopard's gifts to use as his own he is a certain winner.

"I promise," Grey John cries, hoping he'll have enough time to convince Black John that all is not as it seems. He stands up. Moving to his brother's side, he says, "We'll be here," and tugs his brother's arm, pulling him back into their civilised lives, leaving the leopard and the lizard—no! salamander, he reminds himself—where they belong, deep in the primal bushveld ...

#

"... and so you left us here," the leopard ends her recollection, "to start your life's journey. To find your purpose, using only what we each had given you." She pauses, sensing Black John's rising excitement. "Do you remember your promise and what it meant?"

"Yes," Black John says confidently. "Whoever lost tonight would become yours for eternity."

"Are you afraid of losing?"

Black John's laughter howls through the night, stopping even the hyenas as they gnaw their way through yesterday's bones. "How can you even doubt that I've won? Grey John is finished. You can have him," he says callously. "I'm tired of his endless whines. *I'm not giving up yet*," he chants in a parody of his twin's voice. "*There's still hope*." He snorts rudely. "Hope? When even a blind man can see he's just a loser!"

Grey John merely smiles, stroking a tender hand over the salamander's body. "There will be no loser tonight, brother," he says and, with a sigh, lowers the little creature onto a rock. "Goodbye, old friend. Thank you." He's certain the salamander winks at him, before scurrying away into a crevice in the rock.

For a moment, he stands still, gathering his strength inwards. Then he squares his shoulders, swinging round to face the leopard, which has moved closer to Black John. "Take me," he says. "Give him another chance."

"No," the leopard snarls. "You'll be the death of me yet."

"Would that be so bad?" Grey John asks mildly.

"Yes. It must be him. He's been mine for an age." And she looks at Black John with such hunger, such greed, he trembles in shock.

"What's going on?" The thready sound emerging from his throat doesn't sound like a cry of victory, he thinks. "Why does she want *me* when I've won?"

"Oh, you fool!" The leopard's laughter draws the circling hyenas closer and closer. "Do you not know yet?"

"Know what?" Black John's breath hitches in his throat.

"I've had you all along," the Great Watcher says, her eyes glittering with ferocious triumph.

Deep in their voracious depths, Black John finally sees the bitter truth. His life means nothing, nothing at all. It has always been without purpose, without meaning. He's betrayed the better part of himself, not for gold, but for dross.

He turns empty eyes towards his brother. "*You* always had hope." He swallows dryly, his prominent larynx bobbing up and down like a half-eaten apple discarded by children tired of their party games. "But I had none."

Grey John's heart clenches painfully at the sight of his brother's tears. He's seen it coming for years. The disillusionment. The loss of all that he thought he was.

And yet ...

"There is always hope," he murmurs softly.

"Is there?" Black John asks him. "Even for me?"

His brother doesn't know it, but Hope is already alive in his eyes. "Especially for you."

"What about her?" Black John squints at the leopard pacing endlessly round the fire, the swish of her tail almost choking the steadily burning embers into darkness.

"Leave her to me."

The leopard sees him coming and, with all the wrath of one who knows her time is over, she strikes. Once again, she has Grey John by the throat.

This time he's expecting it. Digging his hands into her neck, he keeps the scent of her at bay. In a lascivious parody of fleshly union, they twist and turn, edging ever closer to the flames, which leap and roar into new life even as they wait to consume.

Knowing it is the only way, Grey John boldly steps into the fire, the leopard still clasped to his breast. He holds her there, until defeat and pique fill her eyes. With a sinuous twist, she drags herself from his hold, running yowling into the bushes, ash and burning embers staining her once-beautiful coat.

"You should have killed her!" Black John accuses, as his brother stands up, unharmed by the devouring flames. "Now how can we be safe from her false promises?"

"I will keep you safe," says Grey John, and, as he speaks, his shape begins to shift.

Before Black John's appalled gaze, he changes into a salamander.

"Grey John!" he cries. "Don't leave me!"

"I will never leave you, my brother," the salamander comforts. "Fear not, I will sustain you for I am always in you," and he darts off into the night, leaving Black John alone by the dying fire.

For a long while he stands dazed, and a little bit frightened, until the chill of the night penetrates his trance.

He is one again, and the time has come for him to leave this place. It is time for him to begin to record simple songs long forgotten—the kind that bring joy and hope to a despairing world; songs that will fill his life with purpose.

As he bends to douse the last of the fire's embers with the dregs of his coffee, his reflection in the shiny steel mug captures his eyes. No longer as black as the night, every hair on his head is now an irrevocable cold stone grey.

A Cup of Sorrow

"One spoon or two?"

After ten years of marriage to Fay's brother, would it be too much to expect her to know what I liked? "Black, no sugar, thanks. And I'd prefer a tea bag," I said, "if you have one."

Fay was nothing if not an excellent hostess, always keeping a wide selection to satisfy her guests. Earl Grey or Camomile? With milk or without? she'd ask. Tea bags or tea leaves?

But, for me, there was always only the one question: "One spoon or two?"

She knew I disliked taking that last sip of hot, sweet tea and tasting the grainy leaves hidden in the bottom of the cup.

"I don't have any bags today," she said, scratching around for the tea leaf canister on the second shelf.

I leaned over her short, dumpy frame, easily gathering the tin from the shelf. "Here," I said, and the tin clattered impatiently on the counter.

"Oh, thanks, Sally." She smoothed her apron—the faded yellow one Joe's first wife had made her, years ago before the divorce—and, looking up with a smile, said, "How easy it is for you to reach so high with your long arms!"

Immediately I felt like a white-handed gibbon. So I reached for the box of Five Roses teabags, half hidden behind the full-roast and decaffeinated coffees. "I'll have this instead," I said, "if you don't mind."

"Those are terribly old." She ignored the box in my hand and scooped four spoons of leaves into an old enamel teapot. "And bags just don't have the same flavour as leaves."

Bustling to the stove, she turned the gas on and placed the kettle precisely in the centre of the plate. "The last time I used those old tea bags was when Birget came to visit." She breathed the name of Joe's ex-wife with a nostalgic sigh and gazed out the kitchen window, lost in happy thoughts. Then she sighed again and, although she knew the answer, asked, "You've met Birget, haven't you?"

"Yes," I said, as I had a hundred times before.

"She's such a lovely person." Another sigh, followed by a hesitation so small I almost thought I imagined it, and she added, "She was such a good wife to Joe. I can't deny that just because my brother is married to you now, can I?"

Birgit was so lovely she screwed your brother's best friend, I wanted to remind her, but Fay had never believed that story. She blamed Joe, saying he worked too long hours. She blamed me, saying I enticed him away from his perfect marriage. Never to my face, of course, but as she well knew in our small town gossip had a way of filtering back.

The boiling kettle whistled and she hurried back, pouring the hot water into two mugs through a stained wire strainer. "Birget has three lovely girls now. All under five!" She chuckled. "They keep her looking young."

Adding milk and two sugars to one mug, she said, "Like me, she just loves being a mother. No interest in a fancy book-keeping job for her!"

"I'm Chief Financial Officer of a listed company, Fay, not a book-keeper."

She ignored me. "To think those sweet angels could have been my nieces. Having only boys myself, I would've liked some nieces." With a brave smile, she slid the sugared mug across the counter. "Drink up, Sally. This will perk you up. You look so tired today."

Why did a cup of tea with Fay always end in a cup of sorrow?

"I hate tea made with leaves," I said, "and you know I don't take milk or sugar." I upended the mug in the sink and added, "I'd rather have nothing."

Then I fetched my coat and purse as I left, on that last day I ever accepted Fay's invitation to pop on over for a friendly cup of tea.

The Place of the Doves

"Nkosinathi Mfeka," Nathi said to himself, as he waved goodbye to the disappearing truck and surveyed his treasure, "you are a lucky man!"

In front of his shack, the red-and-grey corrugated iron sheets contrasting with the blue plastic sheet he used as a door, stood a mountain of food. Cartons of milk, boxes of biscuits and tins of beans towered up, almost as high as the Balele Mountains, there near Utrecht where his village lay under the peaks that held the spirits of his ancestors.

Chasing a small grey dove, its round black eyes gleaming with the same hunger that raged in his belly like a summer thunderstorm, Nathi smiled.

In the months since he'd come to the city, he tried hard to find a job, but he'd began to fear his ancestors—the same ones who whispered in his dreams that he'd find gold in the city streets—had lost him. There were so many people here in Diepsloot, how could they not lose him?

But today his luck changed. As the early morning sun coloured the smoke rising over the shantytown a deep rose-pink, he left to seek work and, not a block away, he'd found the truck driver offloading the treasure.

"Help me," the truck driver (clearly a man of stature, for his smart new shoes were as shiny black as his face and his shirt didn't have a single patch) said. "I can't pay you, but you can have all the food you want."

The city had taught Nathi not to be a fool. He touched a discarded carton with his old *takkies*, the toes cut out because they were a size too small. He'd found them in a green trolley bin one long ago Thursday, the day the rich people in nearby Sandton left their rubbish out. "Why don't you want it?"

The driver shrugged. "My boss is clearing his shops. There's a lot where this came from." He grinned broadly; he knew the saliva was already filling Nathi's mouth. "I already have mine," he added.

"How will I get it home?"

"Where do you live?"

"Tlou Street, House Eight Two Two," Nathi said, pointing to the sprawling mass behind them.

"Let's go," the driver said. Between them, it didn't take long to reload the truck.

Soon Nathi was watching the truck leave, its red brake lights blinking farewell.

His hands shaking with eagerness, Nathi opened a packet of biscuits. As he reverently took the first biscuit out, the little grey dove flew down from its perch on the roof of his shack and knocked the biscuits out of his grasp.

As the bright green-and-yellow packet landed in the dust, spilling its bounty, the biscuits became crumbs. The dove started pecking and pecking, making cooing sounds that brought a second dove, then another and another, until all he could see were seething feathers scratching open the boxes and eating his food.

Nathi's shrieks brought his neighbours out. Before he knew what was happening, his mountains of food had become anthills, and the neighbours were disappearing into their own shacks, laden with as much of his treasure as they could carry.

The doves just carried on ravaging the remains. Nathi sank down on his haunches, his elbows resting on his knees. His hands made useless fluttering gestures as he tried to shoo the birds away. In his heart he cursed his ancestors, for giving him a gift and then taking it away again.

One bird, bolder than the others, staggered towards him, peck, pecking the ground frantically. It reached his foot and, just as he feared it was going to peck his toes bloody, it fell over and died with a strangled squawk. One by one, in front of his startled eyes, the other doves collapsed in heaps of feathers, crumbs clinging to their open beaks.

"Look! Look!" he heard someone cry. "The birds are all dead! Nathi wants to poison us!"

When the police came to stop the community from slinging a burning tyre around Nathi's neck, he discovered that the truck driver should have told him the food was bad. If it weren't for the doves, half the community—perhaps even Nathi himself—would have died.

After that day, his neighbours often heard him muttering as he shared whatever crust of bread he had with the doves gathering at his feet.

"Nkosinathi Mfeka," he would say, "You *are* a lucky man!"

The Place of the Doves *was shortlisted for the 2011 African Flash Fiction prize, to be published in* African Writing Issue 12.

Obsession

Food!

Foodfoodfood.

How much there is of it. Everywhere she looks, there are heaps and piles and mountains of glorious, delicious food. Different shapes, different sizes, different colours. What it does for her!

She heaves a deep sigh, breathing in the smells of the spices and the fumes wafting under her nostrils. It conjures up feelings of warm arms; tears wiped away.

"It makes me feel safe," she says.

"Are you afraid?"

"Not me." She hesitates, and then adds in an embarrassed rush. "Not the Cindy of the world. The happy, cheerful soul everyone thinks I am."

I'm puzzled. "Which Cindy are you talking about?"

"The angry Cindy, with her swirling away moods, never solid, always drifting, grasping the edge of life trying to stay sane." She glances at me from wary eyes. "It's that Cindy I feed. And feed and feed and feed."

"But why?" I struggle to understand, for she's always struck me as being an essentially simple soul, as sane as the rest of us pretend to be.

"Sometimes she feels she can be free; but then the fears rise and swallow her. The failures she'll have to face." Cindy sighs heavily. "She wants her life to be different. She wants her life to be the same. But nothing is the same because I'm fat now. And afraid." A hand creeps up to the corner of her eye, pulling the eyelid up and out and down again, up and out and down again. "Sometimes I'm so afraid my brain feels like it's bursting. Until I think of a chocolate bar. Then nothing else matters, except that delicious creamy chocolate." She tugs on her eyelid again, adding with a child's innocence. "Chocolate comforts me. Then it traps me."

Realising what she's doing to her eyelid, she drops her hand, and grips it tightly with the other, as if that's the only way she can keep it still. Suddenly I have an image of a restless, revolting rodent on a wheel, spinning uselessly, trapped in a meaningless, hateful cycle of self-destruction. "Will that Cindy ever break free?"

"I don't know." Her indifferent shrug almost hides the despair. "If she wants to, I suppose."

"Does she want to?"

"It's a slow, horrible suicide," she says abruptly. "It'd be easier for everyone if she took a gun and blew her brains out."

"Who's everyone?"

"Those who need me," she replies. "The ones who eat the other Cindy."

"Eat her?" I want her to keep talking, to see where this is leading.

"Yes." She shifts her bulk uncomfortably, plucking the material away from the heat rash her sliding thighs have caused. "They all want a piece of me. They all want me to make them special; to make them happy."

"Do you feel special?"

"I feel empty. Like I've nothing more to give, not even to those I love."

It's then that I see what she thinks she'll be if she stops eating. She'll simply cease to be; her boundaries are too thin and porous for her to survive in world where even the fall of a leaf fills her with pain and helplessness. I offer her a biscuit from the pack I keep in my draw to reward my young patients. She takes it, laying another solid brick in the wall between Cindy and the world that tosses her aside with such casual cruelty.

Rainbow Farm

(or The Ghost of Christmases Past)

Reading the early edition of the newspaper, Father Christmas bit his nails nervously.
"Rudolph," he said. "What am I going to do?"

Rudolph shook his head sadly as he scanned the advert placed by the new, democratic government. It read:

> **WANTED**
> Rotund, jolly citizen.
> Annual Duties, Sleigh License essential.
> Good elf and management skills needed.
> Affirmative action only.

"Santa," Rudolph sighed, "there's only one thing you can do."

A grateful Santa looked up, saying, "Rudolph, it's always been you that helps me out of a tight spot. What's your suggestion?"

"Simply this—go grabba a tan now!" he replied, his hoof tapping in time to some monotonous TV advertisement ditty that kept running through his head.

"A tan," Santa cried as he looked out the foggy window, "in all this snow?"

He looked around at the bright, white landscape, and at the elves busily working to meet the latest deadline. Their pale skins were slightly flushed with pink as they hurried about trying to cope with an unexpectedly high demand for toys from the New Democracy.

Even Santa, with all his experience, had not seen such thing before. The toys were no different from before; train sets, dolls with pretty clothes and even more guns and warships than usual. As they prepared for the Big Day—the first in the New Democracy—Santa and his elves couldn't help noticing that the orders placed were very much bigger than before.

That was not Santa's worry now. His worry was something far more personal: his job. The only one he knew how to do, and one he had thought secure until the next millennium, when he'd hoped Santa Junior could take over. He had spent years cultivating a delivery system so unique and complex for the toys, only he could organise it. That was why his salary was so high, and the fringe benefits were specially tailored to suit him.

Now, this! Santa could hardly bear to think that after all his efforts Santa Junior wouldn't be able to benefit. He would have to do something; maybe Rudolph's idea wasn't so bad after all.

"A tan?" he repeated, savouring the idea. "But I've always been white, Rudolph, I don't know how to be anything else."

Rudolph—rather callously, Santa thought—shrugged and said "Adapt, or dye, Santa, adapt or dye. It's the only way."

"Die?" Santa replied sarcastically. "What good will that do me?"

"No! No!" Rudolph said shortly, privately thinking that through all the years of working as Santa's main reindeer (without being able share in the fringe benefits) he'd been right in suspecting that Santa was a bit dim. "DYE, Santa, D-Y-E. As in change your colour."

Rudolph's portentous words confirmed Santa's worst nightmare. White wasn't right any more. And, from his snowy white beard to the tips of his shiny white toes, Santa was indisputably, irrevocably white. But Santa, if nothing else, had always had a strong sense of self-preservation. Rudolph was right: if he wanted to keep his job (and all those fringe benefits) he'd have to change his colour.

Conveniently, on the very next page was another advert—but this one appeared to Santa as a godsend. There, before his eyes, was the answer to his problem. "Look, Rudolph, there is a way out after all!"

Rudolph, who by now was busy processing the third copy of the latest batch of toy orders, saved his work and trotted over to Santa's chair to look at what had got Santa so excited.

There was the perfect, instant solution to all of Santa's problems: a special offer for the latest self-tanning lotion. As the ad said, simple, quick and indiscernible from the real thing. Giving, the blurb said, an all-over, even tan.

But nothing, as Santa was about to find out, is ever as simple as it seems.

Being a man who preferred action to theory, he jumped up and decided that as it wasn't a state occasion he didn't need the whole team of reindeer. So, it was enough to hook Rudolph up to the sleigh and leave immediately for the closest Northern Suburbs shopping mall.

He could see by the looks on the faces of the elegantly dressed shoppers that, much like the New Democracy, he had arrived too early for them; none of them were ready for him yet. But he was a man with a mission. Nothing could stop him now—not even the thought of what they would say when he had his tan. His hearty Ho! Ho! Ho! at this notion so startled the lady behind the cosmetics counter that he had to speak to her twice before getting any reply. Waving the newspaper under her disdainful nose, Santa asked for a bottle (with instructions).

"For yourself, sir?" the lady asked, somehow doubting the seriousness of his request.

"No." Santa almost snapped, "For my reindeer."

The bland smile she'd learned during her training course slipped slightly as she said, rather kindly, as if to a lunatic, "This product doesn't work on animal hair, sir, perhaps you should try a pet shop."

Santa's answer to this was so far from what his traditional image dictated he should be the small child standing at the next counter, who'd been watching him with wide-eyed wonder, burst into tears and clutched her mother's skirt, her ideals of what Santa stood for permanently destroyed.

But Santa, in the urgency of his quest, didn't notice the child's distress. Instead, he took a deep breath and smiled stiffly at the young saleslady. Trying to redeem himself, Santa said with grim patience, "That was a joke, dear. It's for me."

The girl giggled nervously. Reaching under the counter, she asked Santa if he knew the rules for applying the solution. He assured her that he would manage—after all, how difficult could it be?

Clutching the answer to all his problems, Santa went back to where he had left Rudolph and shooed away the crowd of interested onlookers, who were listening to Rudolph expound his views on the R.T.P. (for the uninitiated, that stands for Redistribution and Training Programme on how to deliver the toys fairly and equally). Annoyed at the delay, Santa made a mental note to tell Rudolph that speaking to the general public on official matters was unacceptable behaviour for his Chief Animal Aide, however intelligent that Aide might be.

He might not be able to drive his sleigh without Rudolph, but he had to be careful that Rudolph didn't get above himself. That was why he always made sure that Rudolph was excluded from such things as the special fringe benefits package. No use educating the deer—who knew what would happen if Rudolph suddenly discovered education? Why, he might even lead the other deer in a revolt! As Santa indignantly twitched the reins, setting Rudolph in motion, he remembered that it wasn't Rudolph and his fellow workers who were his problem; it was the New Democracy and that advertisement. Giving the chic package in his pocket a satisfied pat, Santa reassured himself that even that problem would soon go away.

How wrong can anyone be?

Looking in the mirror a few hours later, Santa found out as he slowly absorbed the reflection in front of him. His bushy, white beard was as white as ever, and the rest of him was tanned.

Not, however, the beautiful smooth tan that Santa had expected. Before his horrified gaze stood a man, one who had once gloried in his pure white skin, now reduced to something that resembled a Cadbury's Top Deck chocolate.

"Rudolph!" he screeched, giving Rudolph such a fright that his hoof slipped on the keyboard and the data he was working on disappeared into Cyberspace. "Come here, quickly."

Rudolph rushed into Santa's bedroom, anxious to see what the problem was. When he saw Santa he couldn't help but give a choked laugh (actually, it was more of a neighing snort, the kind of laugh you'd expect from a reindeer). The self-tanning lotion did indeed give Santa a tan—but not, as Santa had hoped, a smooth golden brown glow that masked his pasty-white skin. No, Santa's new skin colour consisted of orange and white blotches, all giving off a revealing whiff of chemicals.

Santa was staring aghast at the reflection that stared back at him, moaning softly to himself, "What am I going to do? What am I going to do?"

Rudolph suddenly saw a world of opportunities opening up to him. The ad that had started all of Santa's problems didn't specifically say 'man.' It said 'citizen.' That could mean a man, or a woman, or it could even mean … *a reindeer*!

The more Rudolph thought about it, the better it sounded. He knew the system inside out; he had the loyalty of other reindeers. If he got Santa's job, he would (at last!) be able to access the fringe benefits. First, though, he had to convince Santa that he belonged to the Christmases past.

Trying to look as insouciant as possible (but his heart was secretly racing with excitement at the coming changes), Rudolph turned his attention to the distressed Santa.

"Well!" he said gruffly, his throat clogged with emotion, "Well, Santa, I think this must be the end. This can only mean a golden handshake for you."

"But who'll do my job?" Santa wailed, "It's so close to Christmas already, and I don't want the children to be disappointed!" Despite his faults, Santa was quite a conscientious fellow.

"Don't worry about it, Santa." Rudolph put a commiserating hoof around his shoulders. "They'll find someone; they always do." And, with a barely hidden eagerness, he led Santa out the front door and watched him as he tramped disconsolately out of his warm, cosy office and faded slowly into the empty, snowy wilderness.

Rubbing his hooves together with anticipation, Rudolph thought of all the things he could do to change the lot of the workers, if he got the job. The possibilities were endless—improved training for the elves, better stalls for the reindeer (with heating and running water) and shorter working hours for all.

Taking a deep breath, Rudolph turned to the packed toy factory floor, where everyone had been watching Santa's departure with mixed feelings. Now, they turned their eyes to him.

"Friends, and fellow workers," he began, confidence oozing from every follicle, "all the Christmases to come are going to belong to us. Our time is now! I will reply to the advertisement—but I need your vote! Vote for me, and I promise a better future for us all!"

A great cheer went up and someone started a chant of "Rudolph! Rudolph! Rudolph!" until his ears rang with the echoes of their hope.

With such overwhelming support, there was little doubt in everyone's mind that Rudolph would be the next Santa. Even so, when the announcement came that Rudolph was to be the New Santa Claus, a joyous pandemonium broke out. The elves cried, the reindeer brayed—even the penguins squeaked and the polar bears cavorted in the snow, as they shared in the dreams of their fellow citizens.

As the Big Day approached, the factory was abuzz. This Christmas Day would be different from all the others. No one was quite sure how Rudolph would accomplish the changes, or what they were going to be, but everyone eagerly anticipated that Christmas would never be the same again.

When the time came for the sleigh to be loaded, the reindeer went to collect their harnesses, only to discover that these were not the harnesses of old. Instead, they were beautiful new leather ones, with gold studs and silver bells that jingled every time they shook their heads. They felt so smart and proud in them and, they all agreed, it was all thanks to Rudolph.

The elves, too, couldn't believe their eyes as the sleigh was rolled in for loading. What a magnificent sight it was. In place of the old brown sled, battered after years of use, was a brand new sleigh (an imported German model) with real leather seats (including heating), silver bells (to match those on the reindeer's harnesses) and a boot for toy storage (an extra-large one).

To think that one of their own was driving it. They shivered with excitement, almost incoherent with joy at the thought of the other changes that Rudolph had promised. Changes that he promised would make their lives so much easier, and so much happier. When the New Santa arrived, they decided unanimously, they would raise a cheer for him.

Slowly, the door to the factory opened and they all took a deep breath, ready to raise the roof as Rudolph appeared. And there he was! But the great cheer strangled in their throats, because they were looking at a Rudolph they had never seen before.

He seemed taller, and then they realised that he was standing upright on his two hind legs, balancing precariously on his hooves, on which he had put a pair of black rubber boots.

The biggest difference, though, lay in his fur. Instead of being covered in all that lovely, thick brown fur, there Rudolph stood, dressed in a bright red, fur-lined jacket, a red hat (with a white pom-pom) and long red trousers stuck into his boots.

A collective gasp went up. Dasher turned to Prancer and said in an awe-struck voice, "Look at him. He looks so ... so human!"

Prancer looked at Rudolph, preening at the now silent crowd. He turned his sad, soft-brown eyes onto Dasher. “No,” he said despairingly. “He looks just like the Ghost of Christmases Past.”

They bent their shoulders into the glittering new harnesses and, with a deep groan of effort, they pulled the heavily-laden sleigh forward as the new Santa cracked his whip and chortled “Ho! Ho! Ho!”

Jannie Vermaak's New Bicycle

For thirty long years, Jannie Vermaak rode the same bicycle. His father had given it to him the day he started work at the granary. In summer, he'd offload the corn at the end of the harvest, his child-thin arms soon developing stringy muscles. In the bitter cold of the flatland's winters, he'd earn his pay by catching the rats that came in from the fields for warmth and food.

Once, his bicycle had been beautiful: the deep shiny blue of the sky just before nightfall, with a sunshine yellow stripe down the crossbar and wheels that were big and silvery like the moon. The bicycle was so large his ten-year-old feet could barely reach the pedals. They kept slipping off, so he learnt to stand and pedal all the way down Main Street, with a sharp left turn into Bosman Drive, where the tall round silos of the granary loomed over the edge of the village.

By the time he rode home with his new wife Gladys, the same day they married at the small stone church built on the banks of Wintertown's only river, the yellow stripe on his bicycle had faded to the dull khaki of the mountain grass in winter.

By the time Aunt Sannie died, and her bachelor nephew Gert came to live in Wintertown, Gladys had grown so large she could barely fit on the crossbar and his bicycle had no colour left except for a few patches of blue and the small four-coloured flag of the old Republic.

He'd attached it to the handlebars soon after the war with the English had ended. When he pedalled down Main Street, past Aunt Sannie's General Merchandise Store, where you could buy everything from a needle to the wooden handles of a horse-drawn walking plough, the flag flew straight and proud. Especially at night, when he pedalled as fast as he could to escape the ghost of the abandoned bride, walking the streets of Wintertown looking for her groom.

The missing groom had left his bride standing for days outside the same church in which Jannie had married Gladys. She eventually vanished into the river that trickled past the poor end of town before disappearing into the dryness of the plains somewhere near Doon. Reappearing years later, dressed in her soggy white gown, with mud and reeds trailing from the hem and from her outstretched arms, she searched for a replacement for her lost groom in any unwary man she found.

She'd almost caught Jannie, once, springing out from behind the post office and clutching the handlebars of his bicycle as she'd reached a pale arm up to brush his cheek.

"*Fok*," he'd said, his breath turning whiter than her dress in the frosty air and, his legs now so long that his knees knocked his chin, he'd pedalled home as fast as he could, shocking Gladys as he stumbled in the door and had a shot of *witblits* straight from the bottle he kept hidden beneath his bed for high days and holidays.

After that he never dawdled on the way home, until the day Bachelor Gert rearranged the display in the window of Aunt Sannie's store.

There, in the centre of the pots and pans, the porcelain dolls, rolls of fabric and the rocking chair artfully arranged with a wooden doll dressed in full finery—the latest fashions from Paris in France, Gladys said—there, amidst all the new goods that had the ladies and children in Wintertown oohing and aahing, was a new bicycle.

He fell in love with that bicycle.

It gleamed black, with a large silver bell on the handlebars and white trim on its two sturdy tyres and Jannie longed for it with a passion he'd not felt since first he saw Gladys at the wedding of her second cousin twice removed.

Jannie yearned for that bicycle. At night, he dreamed about it, of how he would look, arriving at work with his new bicycle between his legs, and he dreamed of how he would fly down Main Street so fast that no ghost could catch him.

Gladys started complaining about how he tossed and turned at night. He tried to dream of his new bicycle only when he stopped on the way to work, or on the way home. He'd press his nose against the window and sigh with longing.

Until the day Bachelor Gert was waiting for him, the bicycle out of the window and resting against the door.

"Morning, Jannie," he said. "Why don't you ride the bicycle and see how you like it?"

"I can't afford it," Jannie said, pointing to the £50 sign next to the empty space in the window, half of what he earned in a year. Even as he shook his head, he couldn't resist stroking the handles and feeling the softness of the sleek black saddle.

"Just try it for size," Bachelor Gert said. "You'll soon get used to the hub gear."

Gears? Just like the black-and-gold automobile that the Mayor drove from one end of Main Street to the other when he wanted people to vote for him again, this wonderful machine had gears?

Jannie almost groaned aloud. Before he knew it, he'd swopped his faded old bike and was flying down Main Street, around the corner into Bosman Drive, whipping past the stunned gazes of his friends as they waited for the gates of the granary to open. On he glided, down Stuart Road, under the shadow of the Flat Mountain, until he was back in Main Street, his cheeks red with pleasure and his heart beating with want.

"So?" Bachelor Gert asked when Jannie skidded to a halt in front of him. "Will you be buying it, Jannie?"

"I can't afford it," he almost sobbed, grabbing his old bike back and pedalling furiously away, Bachelor Gert's final words ringing in his ears: "Make a plan, Jannie, and come and talk to me."

That night he did not go to the old featherbed he'd shared with Gladys these past eighteen years.

Instead, he stayed up, sipping slowly from his bottle of whisky until he came up with a plan.

"Come, wife," he said, when Gladys woke the next morning. "Put on your church dress. We are going to town."

"Today's Friday," Gladys said, already in her only other dress, her house dress. "We don't go to town on Fridays."

"We go today," was all Jannie would say, and so Gladys went back into their small bedroom and changed.

Then they were on their way. It was early yet, and there were few ox-wagons on the road. The Mayor's automobile was locked away, because it wasn't election season yet and, as Jannie wobbled past him walking to his office two blocks away from his house, Gladys clung grimly to the handlebars, and said, "Morning, Mr Mayor!"

When they stopped outside Aunt Sannie's General Merchandise Store, she slid off the bicycle with a sigh, stretching her back and straightening her little lace cap.

His new bicycle was still there. Ignoring the questions Gladys asked, he banged on the door until Bachelor Gert opened it with a rush.

He was a fine figure of a man without his striped shop apron, Jannie thought, just as Gladys was a fine figure of a woman dressed in her Sunday best.

"Morning, Gert," he said, before Bachelor Gert could do more than blink. "I've made a plan."

"I thought you would," Bachelor Gert smirked and his eyes drifted over Gladys as she stared into the window at the fashion dummy in those fancy clothes from Paris in France.

"Morning, Mrs Vermaak," he said, and made as if to lift his hat before he realised it was too early and he hadn't yet put it on.

"Morning, Mr Cronje," Gladys replied politely and they both looked at Jannie.

He took a deep breath and thought of his new bicycle. He took Gladys by the hand, sorry for its roughness from all the work of being the wife of a poor man, but still beautiful even though her thin gold wedding band was so much tighter than it had been when he'd first slipped it on her finger.

Holding out her hand to Bachelor Gert, he said, "Gladys cooks good food and she works hard. She keeps a man's bed warm at night. She is a good woman and a good woman is worth her weight in gold." He leaned forward and, picking up Bachelor Gert's limp hand, he joined their hands together. "She is worth more than £50."

"Jannie!" gasped Gladys.

"Mr Vermaak!" said Bachelor Gert, shocked into formality.

Jannie's jaw set stubbornly. "I want my new bicycle," he said and waited.

Bachelor Gert's eyes slowly roved over Gladys and all she offered.

Gladys's eyes sought out first the bicycle her husband hadn't stopped speaking about since first he saw it and then her gaze switched back to the wooden doll still draped in the fancy dress from Paris in France with its flimsy pink material trimmed with glittering buttons and plump white feathers.

"Is it a deal?" Jannie pushed, eager to make the exchange so he could get on his new black-and-white bicycle with its gears and its bell, and be waiting at the gates when the first of his friends arrived for work.

As Bachelor Gert finished inspecting Gladys and she finally pulled her gaze away from the pretty dress, their eyes met with a spark even Jannie felt.

"Yes," they said together. "It's a deal."

And soon the whole of Wintertown grew used to the sight of Jannie Vermaak pedalling his new bicycle down Main Street and greeting Gladys with a cheery wave as, dressed in the finest of fashions from Paris in France, she stood on the arm of her new husband Gert in the open door of Aunt Sannie's General Merchandise Store.

Flash Fiction IV

Winter Skies Waning

"Another new moon," she says,
the darkness once again hiding her tears.
Into the long silence,
he whispers back, "Let's make it a new beginning."

Shelter

Frozen feathers flap
Through a stormy snow-swept sky.
Safe for a moment.

Tiger Bright

Great clawed paws barely breaking a twig, he stays ever vigilant, for he knows the vanity of man destroys that which makes it feel insignificant. To the two-legged beast, seeking power in penile aphrodisiacs and fur coats, the tiger is both beauty and DANGER!

In his strength and his wisdom, he understands their fears.

And so he keeps his beauty and his majesty for when, unseen in the silent shadows of sunlight, he can unleash his full power and simply be free.

The Last Sacrifice

Death stalks I, Rax-ul-can, through the jungle with eyes as cold and yellow as those of the silky black *yaguara*, cat of the night.

I, Rax-ul-can, beloved of the gods, bringer of rain and abundant harvests, Lord of the Four Elements and mighty High Priest of the great city Quchichualxe, welcome death.

Unlike so many others, I do not fear death.

Why should I?

There will be no journey to Zitaltá, the underworld of fire, for me. The gods I have served so well since I was a boy not ten *quin* old will reward me in death as well as they did in life.

Did I not begin with death? My mother died even as I wailed my first cry. Having sacrificed herself to give me life she, too, avoided the fire journey. And, from the incomparable gifts I showed from a young age, she clearly interceded with the gods and our ancestors, who rained their blessings on me from the moment of my creation.

My father, even as he mourned my mother, knew I was destined for greatness.

"Rax, you will have treasures piled higher than the tallest ceiba tree," he would say. "You will be powerful beyond measure. You will have thousands worship at your feet."

"Will I, *Daat*?" I knew he spoke the truth, for I felt the power of the gods within me, but I liked to hear him tell the dream story of my birth night.

"Z'uz'umatz told me so," my father would say, his warm bronze skin weathered by the many seasons he had spent in this world. His voice would deepen with faith and innocence, for he had no doubt the magnificent god Z'uz'umatz himself had spoken as he lay sleeping.

"How did you know it was Z'uz'umatz?"

"By the soaring feathered plumes on his head and the scales on his body; by the red-and-blue feathers on his arms and the forked tongue flickering between the countless teeth in his beak."

"What did he say?"

His hand, calloused from the hours he spent elaborately carving the history of our people into the stone stela, for he was not of noble birth and nor was I, touched my face and he would whisper, "He would tell me that you, Rax-ul-can, will be his greatest *Thizan Qai.* No other High Priest will equal you in skill. No other High Priest will bring as much honour to the gods as you."

So it came to be.

When, at the end of my ninth summer, I entered the walls of the Temple of Cholchun for the first time, I soon became the most favored of all the apprentice *thizans.*

By the time I was fifteen *quin*, my reputation as Skywatcher, and as a superbly accurate thrower of the seeds, had outgrown even my renowned skill at healing the most obscure illnesses.

Kings who were enemies came to our people as supplicants.

"We seek the wisdom of Rax-ul-can," their emissaries would say, as they spread in front of me an untold wealth in *yaguara* pelts, brightly colored forest birds, mounds of corn, and heaps of gold and gems.

I would heal their sons and read their destinies with an easy skill way beyond my youth.

"*Xa i'ik teech atsul*!" They would wish me good luck as they left and, truly, the gods blessed me with the greatest of good fortunes.

Just as Z'uz'umatz had promised my father.

They would also leave behind the daughters of their kings and nobles: to marry or to sacrifice as I saw fit. Only the most beautiful of the maidens paraded in front of me and, on the same day I became *Thizan Qai*, High Priest of the Temple of Cholchun in the great city Quchichualxe, I married my first wife. She was a good woman, for she gave me many fine sons. And Eme-chal.

Aaah. Eme-chal.

If her mother—teeth sharpened and charmingly filled with precious hematite, pyrite, and turquoise—was beautiful, my daughter was a goddess. Her long black hair, her unblemished bronze skin and that most generous gift from the gods: her mother did not have to hang beads over her cradle, for Eme-chal was born with both eyes naturally crossed, a source of loveliness and wonder to all who gazed upon her throughout her life.

On the days of the great festivals, Eme-chal would sit on the sleep chamber floor in my many-roomed stone house, near the centre of the Royal Court—very different from the simple straw-and-mud *cah* I lived in with my father before I became High Priest. Eyes wide with wonder, she would watch her mother prepare me for my duties.

First, there was the scrape of the sharpened obsidian over my skin, cleansing away the remnants of my human sweat and stains. Then would come the fat of the wild pig, scented with jasmine and warmed gently over a fire, before being rubbed over my naked body until it glistened and gleamed like the stars of the sky-gods. The same oil would be combed through my hair, making it shine blacker than the pelt of the *yaguara* as my wife twisted it into a knot tight enough to hold the headdress of a High Priest as exalted as I.

Next, she would wrap the three woven cloths around my loins, the last intricate fold covering my *ph'ok,* my virility, in a soft drape to my knees; then she slipped my feet into sandals made of vine, twisted with threads of fine-beaten gold.

Finally, my primary wife garbed me in the signs of my high office: the long red cloak, the golden collar studded with jewels, and the elaborate headdress, with its lofty macaw feathers of yellow, green, and blue, which would tremble vigorously with even the smallest movement I made.

"Come, daughter," I'd call Eme-chal. Unafraid of my imposing height, and the azure blue tattoos embellishing my face and arms, she'd uncurl herself to run to me with the grace of a deer. Laughing at her eagerness, I'd lift her onto the high wooden table and she would help me slip the golden bracelets with their jangling ornaments onto my wrists. I watched her watch the glittering rewards of my magnificent priesthood: she'd run her chubby fingers over the metal, enraptured by the soft buttery feel.

Her mouth, as tender as the bud of the passion flower, pursed with awe, as I bent my head with deliberate stateliness, making the feathers dance and sway until they tickled her ears and she'd giggle, exclaiming, "*Daat*!"

"*Thizan Qai*!" her mother would correct her. "When he is so dressed, he is not your *Daat*. He is Rax-ul-can, High Priest of the great city Quchichualxe, and all the forests that surround it."

She'd only giggle harder, her baby hands doing their best to capture the swooping feathers of my headdress.

"Your mother is correct," I would say as sternly as I could.

She'd ignore us both and stand high on her toes, reaching up to trace the whirling blue tattoos that adorned my face, before snuggling her head into my shoulder, her tiny hand clutching my arm.

"*Daat*," she'd say, and no admonishment could change her mind.

She kept that possessive grip on me as we walked beyond the streets of our great city and up to the entrance of the soaring pyramid that was the Temple of Cholchun. The tips of her plump fingers played with the bones and feathers dangling from my golden armlets, as if feeling them made her more connected to me as we trudged past the roaring waters of the Sacred Falls, above which I now sit on the temple wall and wait for death. The jungle fell silent as we passed, as if all its wild creatures knew the power of I who walked by.

When we reached the top of the colossal steps leading up to the temple doors, the phalanx of men waiting smiled at the sight we made: the small, beautiful girl-child clinging so lovingly to the arm of her father, their most imposing High Priest.

But even Eme-chal knew she was forbidden to go beyond those massive stone doors the Council of Elders guarded so zealously. No matter how much she implored, no matter what other favours she coaxed from me, she knew I would not take her further than the three-hundred-and-sixty-fifth step.

For beyond that door, carved by her own grandfather, emblazoned with intricate images of the first creation of our people, and framed by two towering stela tapered into bowls in which incense always burned, was the inner shrine where I performed the most sacred, the most holy, of my duties.

For what she did not know, what she could not know, was that beyond that door was where I lifted high the Blade of Faith and offered the bloody hearts of the most beautiful, the most noble souls to one voracious god or another.

#

The roar of a solitary *yaguara* echoed as it leapt out of silence onto an unsuspecting tapir. The jungle that grew thick and lush around the Sacred Falls pressed down on me, and I gasped for my next breath as thousands of voices called to me from the depths of the dark jade waters of the pools beneath the Falls. The voices of the gods called too, whispering that it was not enough, however many souls I'd already sacrificed, it would never be enough to prevent the apocalypse that approached.

My recent visions were stronger with each night that passed.

Eme-chal, my beautiful Eme-chal, had taken to appearing in my dreams as a young child. Her dream eyes filled with mysteries and love, even as her dream mouth poured forth the future's shadowy secrets.

"Canoes, long canoes, bigger even than some of our temples," she said, "are coming to our land from the great ocean flowing under the rising sun."

She told of what she saw in the far off place where she now lived. "Men—no, not men—gods, twice taller even than you, *Daat*, when you are dressed for the great festivals. White woven cloths tied above their canoes capture the breath of the gods, driving them to our shores. Their faces, half covered in thick black hair, are as bronzed as ours. But beneath their strange silver breast plates, their bodies glow whiter than the light of the moon goddess as she rides the full moon through the dark heavens."

In my dreams, and when I woke remembering her words, I shook my head in disbelief. Such pre-eminent men could surely not exist?

"These strange peoples bring death," Eme-chal whispered the next night, and the next.

"I do not fear death," I said.

"They bring destruction," she moaned.

"Destruction is already upon us," I said, thinking that it was when she was a child but fourteen *quin*, her loveliness already overshadowing the soft beauty of the sacred frangipani, that the gods had begun to desert me.

She had no memory of that year, nor the death and destruction that followed as I offered the gods more and more blood sacrifices to appease the anger that had so suddenly overtaken them. For surely they were angry beyond compare when they no longer granted me what I most longed for?

"Just one more sacrifice, *Daat*," my dream Eme-chal sighed. "Just one last sacrifice." Her languorous hands reached out, baby fingers curling as they had once curled around my armlets as we walked up the stairs to the temple. "All your doubts will be gone, swallowed up as the mist of the morning swallows up the great Temple of Cholchun. All your fears, too, will melt as the mist melts when Ah Q'uatchil wakes his sun chariot and, once more, you will know only the love of the gods, not their anger."

At first, I ignored her dream voice; such a sacrifice—a single soul—would not appease the gods' displeasure when all the sacrifices I had made in the last ten *quin* had not satisfied them.

Not even the Festival of Blood had satisfied them. They had not heard my pleas then, nor granted my request. Could one sacrifice do what all the others had not?

The Festival of Blood.

The thought of it still burned through my veins until I could no longer sit in the contemplative pose I'd held for more hours than I could remember, here at the Sacred Falls next to the Temple of Cholchun, my sanctuary for almost a lifetime. Uncrossing my legs, I stood without needing aid from the dozen *thizans* who waited silently for my commands. The younger neophytes, not yet schooled in masking their reactions, showed veneration at my feat. I was secretly proud that, even at my age, my movements had barely set the feathers in my headdress quivering.

I stood as tall and sturdy as the old ceiba tree I'd planted to thank the gods the day Eme-chal was born. When the blood tingled to life in my feet again, I stepped over the old straw doll that I'd woven for her—her favorite toy until the day she went from virgin daughter to honorable woman.

#

She'd never been more beautiful than when I lead her to her destiny.

I'd never forgotten that day. The holy marriage of Rax-ul-can's only daughter was a day to celebrate before the entire city.

The sun god Ah Q'uatchil shone his pleasure on us, adding radiance to the excitement, the eagerness, lighting Eme-chal from within. Trust and faith, in both her father and her gods, to guide her true, added a divine glow to her golden skin.

That day ten summers ago I, too, shared both her trust and faith, for then I was still the gods' favoured one: I was Rax-ul-can, beloved of the gods, bringer of rain and abundant harvests, Lord of the Four Elements and mighty High Priest of the great city Quchichualxe, obedient servant and faithful believer.

And yet I have been empty of both faith and trust since that day I gave my Eme-chal away.

What father wants to give his beloved daughter to another, never to see her again?

Nothing the gods gifted me with after that day could fill the void left by Eme-chal's absence.

No sacrifice I made to the gods helped me.

Not even the Festival of Blood stopped the stuttering of my heart, as it yearned for my daughter, virgin no longer but now a wedded bride.

#

"Twenty thousand virgins," I said to the Lord Warrior, when he asked what I thought would appease the gods' anger in the fifth season of poor harvest after Eme-chal had left.

"With respect, *Thizan Qai,*" he bowed low, his fingers curling tightly around his bow to stop their shaking as he feared my displeasure. "How can you sacrifice *twenty thousand* maidens in four days?"

"Per day," I corrected him, holding my face as impassive as the stones in the temple when he blanched. I'd not forgotten how he'd laughed and staggered around, drunk with delight and honeyed *b'ocolatl,* the day I said goodbye to Eme-chal. I threw a challenging look around the Council of Elders, the leaping flames of the fire they circled highlighting their aged faces, more deeply lined with worry as they debated a way to end the poor harvests that continued to bring our faltering nation to the edge of starvation.

"Eighty thousand virgins in total? That's impossible! The Lord Warrior could never capture so many before the Festival of the Sleeping Sun," said the eldest of the council members.

"Nothing is impossible," I said, "when it's done on the command of the gods."

I met his eyes then, careful to keep all the emptiness in my soul well hidden. He, too, had taken too much pleasure at the sight of Eme-chal in her wedding finery. "Is that not what you told me once? Before Eme-chal's holy marriage?"

His gaze dropped first and, with a curt laugh, I kicked sand into the fire, killing the light, as I reiterated my command to Yum Xipe, Lord Warrior of the nation's armies.

"I have read the signs in the skies. You have three moons to bring the necessary sacrifices. None older than fourteen *quin*. All must have pure blood, or the gods will remain unforgiving."

What a fool I was!

Why did I still believe that the gods cared about us? They had long forsaken us. Even I, Rax-ul-can, most preferred of their priests, was no longer favoured.

Within three moons, I had my eighty thousand maidens. As the moon goddess drew a cloak across the face of the sun god and brought night at midday we started the sacrifices.

For four days, the halls of the temple rang with the sound of dozens of blades, slicing and cutting. Rivers of blood flowed down the temple steps, turning the waters of the Sacred Falls from jade to red as every council member, every nobleman, even the youngest *thizan*, made sacrifice after sacrifice until Festival of the Sleeping Sun became known as the Festival of Blood.

The stench of death filled our city for weeks.

But the greatest stench came from inside me, for it was only then, as I waited and waited amongst the decaying piles of young girls, that I finally knew my gods had betrayed me.

I had not lost my faith when I could no longer bring the rains. I had not lost my trust when I could no longer bring victory after victory to our warriors.

I had not even stopped believing in the gods' favour ten summers ago when I walked Eme-chal up the stairs and, for the first time in her young life, allowed her to pass through the great stone door into the inner shrine of the Temple of Cholchun, where I performed my most holy duty as High Priest.

I still believed in their promises even as, in the smoky half-light I stripped her bare and spread-eagled her on the stone altar, binding her arms and her legs with vines her mother had woven. I daubed her with *azul*, the sticky mix of clay and indigo añil shining wetly on her naked limbs as the straw torches burned as feverishly as the lascivious eyes of her waiting bridegrooms, the fierce faces of the gods painted on the ceiling and the walls.

As I smoothed the last stroke of paint around the gate of her purity, the *thizans* carried the bowl of precious honeyed *b'ocolatl* to Eme-chal. She drank her fill then I, and the waiting Council of Elders, emptied the bowl. Soon the flames became faces and the humming in our heads became visions. We began the sacred bloodletting, calling the ancestors' spirits, praising the gods with howls of rapture as the bone spikes lacerated our bodies.

It was my duty as Rax-ul-can, father no longer but the most High Priest of the Temple of Cholchun, saviour of our peoples, forever to bind my Eme-chal in sacred union with the gods themselves.

I danced closer and closer to the sacrificial altar, chanting the age-old vows, blood running from my ears, my tongue, and my nipples. With a scream of agony, I pierced my *ph'ok* and, with one thrust, filled her with all the virile power the gods had endowed me. The blood of her maidenhood sprang forth, uniting with the blood of the gods pouring forth from my *ph'ok.* The consecration of this holy union had begun.

My Eme-chal did me proud that day of her marriage to the gods of our people.

She flinched, but not once did she cry out; not even as the Council of Elders—as was expected by virtue of their worldly representation of the gods—took their turn clambering up the altar to mix their bleeding *ph'oks* with Eme-chal's fragile soul. She lay there, accepting her sacred destiny with all the nobility of her young heart. She showed no fear. Her eyes, dazed from the honeyed *b'ocolatl,* were wide with trust and love, and clung to mine all through the ordeal of this sacred marriage ceremony as her multitude of priestly husbands, each representing one of our gods, took his turn at that torn and bloodied gate.

When the youngest *thizan*, younger even than she, had finished, she lay still, believing in the gods, believing in *me*, because I had told her this sacrifice, this marriage to the gods of her body and of her soul, was what the gods needed to save us all.

I gave her a small nod of approval and as I stepped up to the altar and laid my hand on her tender thigh, bloodied with the mix of blood and priestly power, my brave girl allowed the first flicker of pain and relief to creep into her beautiful eyes.

It was then I felt the first of my doubts that would ultimately consume me, yet I dipped my hand between her thighs to scoop up the holy fluid and, around her budding breasts, drew a circle on her chest, a circle that marked the site of her living heart. I kept my hand there, feeling the slow thud, and waited for the gods to show me their favour.

When they remained still and silent, I knew they were not yet satisfied.

I raised high the Blade of Faith. The flames of the torches lighting the cavernous hall glimmered wickedly over its obsidian sheen and, as we had just joined her body with that of the gods, I prepared to join her soul with theirs to save our people.

The chants from around the altar changed pitch, reaching a crescendo and, with my faith guiding me—or blinding me—I struck straight and true, the blade sinking so deep into Eme-chal's bone and flesh, the shock reverberated up my arm, rattling the bones and feathers she had so liked to cling to.

With my skill and the strength developed after so many years as High Priest, I worked quickly. The fading light of trust still shone in her eyes even as I held her wildly beating heart high above my headdress and sang my prayers to the gods who watched over us.

The *thizans*, squealing with excitement, sliced through the plaited vines holding her to the altar. They carried her to the very edge of the wall of sacrifice, beneath which all the people of our great city, drunk on the common c*albhé* and their hope, waited along with the gods, her Divine Husbands, and threw her body and heart over the Sacred Falls into the pools far below.

As the purifying waters embraced her with thundering haste—or perhaps that was the hungry gods welcoming her—I couldn't help but throw a triumphant glance at the Council of Elders, as if to say, "You're right. Nothing is impossible!"

For when they first came to me, complaining that my rituals no longer worked and my predictions were inaccurate, that the gods had removed us from their favour, I had laughed at them and said, "Never. All the gods need is the right sacrifice. I will find the most beautiful, the most pure bride alive and the gods will return to shower us with their gifts."

"Eme-chal," someone had called. "Eme-chal is the one the gods want."

"Impossible!" I'd shouted, leaping to my feet and waving my fist in the direction of the faceless voice. "Eme-chal is my daughter! My only daughter! To sacrifice her would be impossible!"

"For you, Rax-ul-can," the calm voices of the Council continued, "For you, a High Priest so honoured by the gods that the great god Z'uz'umatz himself appeared at your birth, nothing is impossible."

So it came to be.

Throughout the week of fasting leading to Eme-chal's wedding day I believed nothing was impossible. I believed, too, that the gods would stay my hand with some magnificent sign from the heavens. Even as I held high the Blade of Faith, I trusted that they would somehow bring my Eme-chal back to me, her body whole and pure again, her face alight with love.

From the day I watched Eme-chal's heart slowly stop beating in my hand, I had searched and searched for the one gift that would show the gods how worthy I was. For I believed that, if I gave them what they desired, if they wanted to honour me beyond imagination, they could give me one small gift in return: my Eme-chal.

With every sacrifice, with every *quin* that passed, my faith dimmed, for still the gods did not return her. It was two summers ago that I realised the gods needed more, much more, than they had ever received before.

When I read the sky charts and saw the coming of the Sleeping Sun, I knew that such an auspicious heavenly event would be the perfect time to hold a festival so enormous, sacrifices so unprecedented, that the selfish gods would send my Eme-chal back at last. Surely, I believed, even for the angriest of gods, eighty thousand brides would be enough of an exchange for one small daughter?

But, as the days after what became known as the Festival of Blood passed, and the thousands of bodies rotted on the stairs of the temple and in the waters of the Falls, all but the last remnants of my faith rotted and decayed too.

Until Eme-chal, with her dream murmurs of the annihilation awaiting my people in the near time, came to me in my dreams and spoke to me of the last sacrifice.

#

I shook myself from my trance and moved to the very edge of the Sacred Falls, next to the low wall over which I had seen so many noble sacrifices plunge. My headdress quivered and the youngest *thizan*—my grandson, eldest son of my eldest son—laughed with delight. He knew how those feathers could tickle.

Because he reminded me so much of Eme-chal, I smiled at him.

"Come," I said, calling him over in a voice softened by memories of my daughter. My eldest son made a sound of protest, quickly silenced with a look. I called my grandson again. "Come, boy, you shall honour the gods and your ancestors by helping me. Bring the honeyed *b'ocolatl* and let us drink."

His small face alight with pride and effort, he hurried to stand next to me, his head barely extending above the wall of sacrifice and I began the preparatory ritual I had done so often.

I drank from the painted bowl to take my mind into the vision world; I pierced my nose and my ears, so I could more clearly hear the voices of the gods as they guided the Blade of Faith. Finally, I pierced my *ph'ok*.

My holy blood ran free and fast. With my left hand, the one Eme-chal had loved to hold so tightly, I dipped into the pool of my blood and drew a perfect circle on my chest. With my right hand, I lifted the Blade of Faith as high as I could. I gave the *thizans* the signal and their chants echoed through my head as I shouted the words of my final offering and slammed the obsidian blade deep into my chest.

With the gods' strength keeping me upright and the voice of my daughter urging me on as she called from the dark, dark pools below, I finished the slice and cut. For the good of my people, I tore out my still beating heart, offering the last sacrifice to my gods.

Only then did I surrender and let myself tumble over the low temple wall into the icy waters of the Sacred Falls. A terrible dimness overtook me and, at last, I joined my Eme-chal where she waited, forever embraced in the arms of the gods whom I had loved and served so well.

The Last Sacrifice *first appeared in* The Fall: Tales from the Apocalypse *published by The Elephant's Book Shelf Press (USA) in November 2012.*

Now I Know

To Simon, there is nothing as satisfying as the resounding clash of cymbals. When the halves meet in their passionate embrace of echoing brass, he closes his eyes in an ecstasy he can find nowhere else.

"Simon!" Mary, his wife, hisses from the corner of her mouth. "Stop that!"

Simon's uninhibited reaction strikes her as obscene in a man of his intellect. The little moan he makes scares her. It hints at a lack of control, a passion out of sync with the sophisticated academic mind that so draws her to him. It's messy, that little grunt, and Mary doesn't like messy.

"Stop what, love?"

"That noise you make when the cymbals clash."

"Oh." A touch of red creeps from his collar, and he tugs at his latest bow tie. Yellow with tiny navy anchors, it's unlike any other in his vast collection.

Bow ties are the one passion Mary can't wean him from. Eventually, giving in with good grace, she now treats it as an endearing, eccentric quirk of his genius. She bought him this little gem, liking the multitude of anchors, lying solid and somehow dignified on their sea of yellow silk.

"Sorry," he says, but he doesn't mean it. The cymbals speak to him with an intensity he hasn't experienced since he first fell in love with Mary. "The new percussionist is good, isn't she?"

"A bit young," Mary says, sounding relieved now that he's returned to safe waters. "Her inexperience shows."

Of course it does, he wants to say. She's young—too young—for the thoughts he has every time she opens her arms wide, smacking the cymbals together, her face ablaze with joy.

Had he ever been so young that he felt so deeply?

The young cymbal player, her carrot hair and freckles giving her passion an odd innocence, reminds him of the first heady days he was married to Mary …

#

"I've found it, Mary, love," Simon shouted, startling her out of a dreamy contemplation of her slightly rounded stomach, wondering when she'd feel the first kick, the first flutter of life of their first child.

"You couldn't have," she said placidly. "You know the Riemann hypothesis is unsolvable. What happened to your hair?" His pony tail had come loose from its rubber band and his thick, black hair lay rumpled about his face. "You look more like one of your students. You'll need to cut it before the baby's born."

"Yes, yes," Simon muttered, as he flung himself down on the grass beside her. "But look here, Mary, do you see how the real part of any non-trivial zero of the zeta function …" and he was off, into the abstract realms of his mathematics, in ways she could never hope to understand, so she let herself drift away again, tuning in to the fire in his voice, the lust for answers that burned away all the food he ate. He always looked half-starved; he had from the day she first saw him at the student protest against increased student fees.

He'd been on the platform, rattling off calculations and the projected effects of the fee increase with an intensity that had drawn her and other passing students into the protest, even though most of them hadn't understood what he'd been saying. It hadn't mattered then, because his fire had swept them all along to the first student victory on the campus.

Closing her eyes, she relished the cool breeze on her cheeks and the mild spring sunshine on her bare arms. His voice became a soft babble in the background and she made the occasional sound of agreement, thinking about the new curtains she wanted to buy now that they'd moved into their first house. Simon had wanted to wait for a baby. His dream had been to apply for two years sabbatical to work and study his mathematics at Stanford University in America.

"This is more important," Mary said, when she told him about the baby. "What good does maths do in the world?"

His voice rising and falling with excitement, he'd started on about the pure beauty of numbers, of the truth they contained in their simple austerity, but half-way through she'd had her first bout of morning sickness.

When it was over, and she sat shaky and still nauseous on the small bathroom floor, he ripped up the application form. "We can go later," he said, "when the baby's bigger."

#

They never did get to go to Stanford for the sabbatical, because somehow his salary had always gone on bond payments or school fees or a new station wagon instead of the old Mini Cooper he'd loved.

Dear Mary. A few years ago, she'd surprised him by bringing him a newspaper cutting about the Millennium Prize Problems.

"Here's your chance," she'd said, brushing her hand over his close-cropped hair, more silver than black now. "The Riemann hypothesis is still unsolved! And you can win a million American dollars for solving it."

He'd leaned back in his study chair, adjusting the foam cushion he used to help the constant back ache he had since he'd gained a little weight. Taking the cutting from her, he'd glanced at it before sliding it under the pile of student papers he had to mark. "I'll look at it when I'm finished with these," he'd said.

He hadn't thought about that cutting or his dream of solving the unsolvable prime number problem for years now.

But when the young girl brought the cymbals together, her face full of joy in the simple act, a part of him yearns for that same satisfaction; aches to sigh the same sigh of ecstasy puffing her cheeks. What does she feel? Do all her dreams come alive, woken from the slumber of mediocrity, at the very moment she gives the cymbals another single solid smack?

Mary's elbow in his ribs brings his startled gaze downwards. "It's over, Simon. Applaud!" Her frown stays in place as she joins the rest of the audience in the polite clapping.

Mechanically, Simon joins in, his left palm meeting his right in a puny sound so resembling his life. In principle, clapping hands is the same as clapping cymbals, but the restrained sound of his palms arouses nothing more than a mild annoyance. What he wants to do is shout and stamp his feet, to twirl round and round in the outburst of passion—of joy!—the girl's cymbals conjure up; but in a life ruled by reason, he can't commit the unforgivable sin of being out of control.

When they arrive home, his soul is still feverish.

"Mary ..." Her name falls from his lips in a way reminiscent of their early days together, before familiarity and responsibility took their toll. Putting his hands around her waist, not much thicker than when he first kissed her, he says again, "Mary …"

In the pounding of his blood, the cymbals soar as Mary leans back into his embrace. With a gentle firmness he knows is unrelenting, she says, "It's late, Simon. Tomorrow's a work day." She gives him a consolation kiss, not so much full of promise as full of comfort. "Let's wait until Saturday. We'll both be fresher; more able to enjoy it."

Saturday's too late, he wants to cry out. But all he says is, "Of course, love," and beneath his sensible acceptance of her sensible refusal, the sound of cymbals crash and roar in his head.

The next day, guilty and a little remorseful for the thoughts he has lying awake listening to Mary's familiar soft snores, he sends her a bunch of flowers. On impulse, he also sends lilies—bright orange tiger lilies, as passionate as her performance—to the young percussionist.

#

"Professor Miles?"

It isn't a voice he recognises. He looks up and sees a young woman standing at his desk, slender in casual jeans and a lime-green blouse, a cap pulled low over her eyes.

"Can I help you?" Young as she is, she's still older than his usual students.

"No." A smile flickers and, without asking, she pulls out a chair. For some unknown reason, the few faint freckles on her hand set his heart pumping. "But I can help you."

Simon puts the churning inside him down to irritation. He has a paper to present next month and he has yet to complete it. Cryptic interruptions are not what he needs.

"I doubt it." He shuffles the papers on his desk in a broad hint.

"I can give you the answers to your problems. I can give you life."

Her voice, soft as it is, brings with it a gust of fresh air and he freezes in mid-shuffle. Slowly he lifts his gaze, up past the freckled hand, lying open and relaxed on the chipped arm of his visitor's chair. How had he missed that abundance of freckles on her cheeks and nose? Or the strand of bright hair curling from under the jaunty cap?

Between one breath and the next he is young again.

"You already have," he says. "Your performance last week was ... breathtaking."

She laughs.

The last time he'd heard such a joyful sound—soul-deep and full of passion—was when she crashed her cymbals together. Closing his eyes in ecstasy, he lets it roll through him.

"Thanks." She leans forward, her young, unfettered breasts thrusting high against the material stretching across them. "How did you know where to send the flowers?"

"I phoned the city offices, who gave me the name of your conductor, who..."

"... gave you my address." Shifting in her seat, she sends him an indecipherable look. "He shouldn't have."

"I convinced him."

"So you did." She smiles. "He said you were very passionate."

Taken aback, for he didn't think he knew how to be passionate about anything any more, he exclaims, "Me?"

Nodding, she says, "That's why I'm here. Your passion." She strokes a short-nailed finger, surprisingly square, across the edge of her smile. "And what you said in your card."

Unable to hold the temptation he sees in her gaze, he drops his own to the papers he still holds in his hand. "Your playing—" He clears his throat, embarrassed at his emotions. "Your playing makes me feel alive again."

"So you said in your note." Her smile broadens and his heart pumps new life into his veins. "I can feel that you're still very much alive."

"Not always," he whispers. "Not for a long time."

In the silence following his words, his office goes from small to claustrophobic. "Do you find it hot in here?"

Without waiting for her reply, he jumps up to push open the window. The ritual of holding the handle with one hand, while jabbing at the stuck corner with the other, calms him. "There," he says, satisfied, as the window stutters open.

Taking a deep breath, he turns to face her again, not knowing what he wants to say until he sees her brown eyes, sparking with life and laughter.

"Would you have lunch with me?" She looks at him quizzically and, so she doesn't misunderstand him, he adds, "In the campus canteen. It's busy at this time of day."

Her head tilts to one side, a bit like the orange-breasted Cape Robin he feeds each morning, considering how dangerous he is before hopping forward and gracefully nipping the bread crust from his fingers.

"Do you eat Italian?"

"I used to." When he was younger. Mary has an allergy to pasta, so he rarely eats it these days.

"Good!" She says and in one lithe movement stands up, slinging her purse over her shoulder. "I know a place near here. Their pasta is ... mmmm, *magnifico*!" She kisses her fingertips and laughs at her bad imitation of an Italian accent.

He fancies her freckles dance and a wave of answering heat rises in him. Striving to keep his dignity—for this close, the gap in their ages is even more obvious—he gives a restrained smile at her clowning. "It'll be my pleasure."

Such a mundane act, he thinks, asking a woman to lunch. Yet, it's different, so different. The curl of longing in his belly has an intensity he's not felt since his youth.

Reaching for his jacket, he checks his wallet is in place, using the simple action to steady the roar of cymbals echoing in his soul. Until, with the old-fashioned courtesy Mary likes so much, he touches his hand to the girl's elbow and says, "Shall we go?"

#

Three months after that first simple lunch, Simon still remembers what they ate. *Penne Alfredo*, the smooth taste of the cream and ham contrasting pleasantly with the crusty bread and heavy red wine. But what he remembers most about that lunch, and all the others since, is the laughter.

In the same way she plays her cymbals, the girl holds nothing back from her dance with life. It makes Simon content every time she lets her freckles jive to the music of her laughter.

"You're happy these days," Mary says. "Is work going well?"

"Everything's going well, love!" In a rush of emotion, he hugged her tightly, something he'd forgotten to do in recent years.

There's a flare of confusion in Mary's eyes.

"Are you getting a promotion?"

He laughs and does a quick two-step, leading her away from the sink. He doesn't tell her the Dean called him in to say he's missing too many afternoon lectures. How can he explain to the Dean that, when he's with Charity, time has no meaning?

"Does it have to be something?" he asks, and nuzzles his wife's neck.

"Not now, Simon!" She raises hands covered in lather and nods to the dishes piled high on the table. "I shouldn't have left them until this morning."

He leaves her with her soapsuds and her thoughts.

Yesterday evening went well, Simon entertaining their guests with a wit she hasn't heard since he was young.

That's it! she realises. *That's* how Simon's changed.

He's shaken off his mantle of maturity, behaving as exuberantly as a teenager doing the twist. It's as if he's got some secret knowledge, some hidden vision, which fills him with joy. It worries her, how he whistles all the time. Sometimes he chuckles to himself, and then his eyes glaze and she knows he's gone away, to some secret place she can't follow.

She knows he's a dreamer. For all his academic brilliance, there's a streak of the irrational in Simon. His mathematical genius lay in his way of going inward; into a world of his own from whence spring the visions that resolve irresolvable theorems.

For years, he lost his genius: or so she thought. Until recently, when he's reverted to the man she knew during their courtship. His eyes glow with the excitement of new discoveries, his feet never far from the soft shuffle of some solitary rhythm in his head. She smiles tenderly, remembering those early days when they were in love ... *in love!*

She freezes, up to the elbows in dirty dishwater. He was letting his hair grow longer. He was running again, losing some of the weight he'd picked up. The suppressed excitement, always greatest on Mondays and Wednesdays. Most importantly, the return of his genius: last week she'd seen him reading his old papers on the Riemann hypothesis. So many clues, she wonders how she missed them before.

She waits until her churning emotions have calmed, but it's not long before she decides what to do: she'll fight for him.

Her weapons are formidable. She's still attractive. She's intelligent and she knows Simon well. If she has to, she'll use the children, for Simon loves his boys. No mid-life crisis will change that.

Then, she'll find out who the young woman is. Simon's lover must be young, for he's at that age when men need to prove their virility. Her mistake was assuming Simon too intellectual to follow the frailty of his body.

Fortified by her plans, she briskly wipes her hands and removes her apron. In the guest bathroom, she dabs some perfume on her wrists, and examines her reflection in the mirror relieved it confirms her mature good looks. Then she follows Simon into his study. Listening to his Bose, he's lying back in his chair, with stereo headphones on. The volume seeps through the heavy plastic and, faintly, she hears the clash of cymbals.

Simon's smile disappears as she switches it off with something of a snap. When he lifts the headphones she's under control again and, before he says a word, carries out her plan.

"You were wonderful last night," she says. Cupping her hands around his cheeks, she registers his surprise. "The dishes can wait."

She bends forward, sealing his lips with hers, slowly deepening the kiss until his hands, stiff with awkwardness—but soon loosening into eagerness—rise to grasp her waist. The sound of cymbals forgotten, he pulls her onto his lap, and she laughs with quiet satisfaction.

#

She sees them together the following Monday. The woman looks young—too young—and a tremor of alarm runs through her. Simon is not someone she expects to be predictable, not with his huge intellect. Her disappointment in him grows.

They're sitting at a small corner table, an array of empty glasses crowding around a faded plastic flower. Fighting down her panic, she dismisses the waiter with a basilisk stare and marches across to stand behind her husband's shoulder.

The girl looks up first. She's surprisingly plain, and Mary's panic subsides of its own accord. Then the girl smiles at her, looking somehow familiar, and Mary hears the faint sound of cymbals.

"Hello, Simon," she says. He looks up and she's dismayed to realise the recognition in his face is not of her voice, but of his name. "Are you going to introduce me to your friend?"

"Mary!" His chair clatters back and all she sees on his face is surprise, and a disappointment he can't hide quickly enough. "What are you doing here?"

She ignores his question, and the young woman's tentative smile. "This is over, Simon. Come home."

"Later," he says, and his chin juts stubbornly.

"Now." The tremor is back, an earthquake. She's almost ashamed to use her greatest weapon so soon in this battle. "The boys need you. Don't throw it away on *her*."

She still doesn't look at the girl and sees understanding dawn in his eyes.

"Mary, love," he touches a tender finger to the frown lines between her eyes, and says, "you've no need to worry. Charity isn't what you're thinking."

"Oh?" She doesn't bother to hide her disbelief. His secretary told her where they'd be, the pity in her gaze galling to Mary's pride. "What is she then?"

"She gives me life."

"Talk sense, Simon!"

"Charity shows me how to feel again; how to live and how to be alive." His voice is deep and husky, passionate as he tries to convince her. "I can dream again."

"Nonsense! Dreaming is for children."

"Don't you want to dream any more, love?"

"One has to be sensible, Simon."

"*All* the time?"

Her nod is relentless, and then she smiles shakily, holding out her hand, the one flashing her wedding ring. "Come home with me. Forget this."

He knows her well, seeing the strain, and the fear, in her smile. "I can't," he says regretfully. "Not yet." He winces as the pain seeps into her so-loved eyes and tries to make her understand. "This isn't an affair." He looks at the young woman, who nods solemnly.

Mary glances at her, seeing the same light of life that's in Simon's eyes, and a great calm descends on her, growing into the crash of cymbals. As a roar surges through her blood, a long-forgotten image of her own childish hopes and dreams is born in the girl's eyes. Joy almost explodes in some forgotten corner of her heart.

She shakes her head to clear it. With her usual rigid resolve, she finally banishes the unusual whimsy threatening to overwhelm her. In the silence that follows, she asks waspishly, “What is it then?”

“It’s about hope.” He stops, shrugging helplessly, unable to find the words to explain what Charity gives him. “It’s about love unstained by this world of desire ... it’s pure and perfect and innocent.”

“Nothing’s perfect or innocent any more.” Even if the girl’s freckles do give her a wispy wholesomeness, Mary refuses to believe what her heart is telling her. How can Simon be so stupid, risking all he has for the illusion of innocence? “Think about what you’re doing. This will end,” she prophesises reasonably, “and you’ll have nothing left. You’re making a mockery of the way you’ve lived your life.”

“Before Charity,” he says, looking at her strangely, “I never saw anything clearly. Now I know what I seek.”

“What’s that?”

“Love ...” he breathes, and smiles brilliantly at her, his dark, usually dour face, alight with something she doesn’t understand. “Charity ...”

She closes her eyes as foreboding clutches her, wondering if she’s already lost the war.

“I’ve learnt how to love again.” He grasps her shoulders, pulling her nearer as he rests his forehead on hers. Looking deeply into her troubled eyes, he says, “Can’t you see, Mary? I’m nothing without Charity, nothing but a mask without a soul.”

“No-o-o ...” The cry of loss escapes Mary before she can stop it. Then she gathers her strength and pulls out of his arms. She rubs her hands down her cotton skirt until she’s certain her face is clear of all emotion. “Come home with me.”

It’s an outright order, but she doesn’t care anymore. All that matters is that Simon is lost to her. He’s stopped thinking and has allowed his emotions to destroy all he was, and all she is.

“You’ve nothing to worry about,” he promises. “I’ll come later, when I know more about Charity.”

“You’ll come right now, Simon.” Her voice hardens. “Or the boys and I won’t be waiting for you when you do get home. I’ll give you five minutes to say goodbye.”

Ignoring the girl, she turns, heading for the exit without a backward glance, her back ramrod straight with bitter pride.

In Simon's head the cymbals clang and bang in a sad cacophony, almost drowning out what Charity says to him.

"Go to her, and tell her what you've learnt."

"She'll never understand."

"She might."

"Not Mary," he says. "She's afraid of life. Of love."

"So were you." She smiles, and his heart lifts. "Mary can learn not to be."

"She might," he agrees, but they both know he's lying.

"Will you remember me?"

"I need you," he says, not moving.

He thinks of nights past, long, dreary nights, listening to Mary's snores, and his thoughts. The wicked ones, the ones reminding him of a life lived in ecstasy, before marriage and age and reason sucked the passion from them, killing all their dreams.

Mary's grown comfortable with the calm seas of their ordinary life. So how can he tell her his soul dulls and dies at the thought of leaving what this child offers him?

But Charity doesn't fail him. He looks at her, and sees wisdom beyond any knowledge he has gathered through the years. *Even as I know her, she knows me*, he realises. *I am flawed and yet still she loves me.*

Certainty swells his heart: in an instant, he knows how to love Mary again.

"Go to her," Charity says, smiling as she sees understanding dawn in his eyes. "You don't need me any more."

He knows she speaks the truth and the gift she gives so generously binds them forever, easing the choice he will make. Leaning down, he kisses her freckles. "Thank you," he murmurs and turns away, strong and free.

He walks towards the shadow of his wife, waiting beyond the door, knowing Charity will never leave him. She lives on, deep inside the secret raptures of his heart.

Mary turns to greet him, stroking his tie in welcome. It's her favourite. Today the little navy anchors are the most welcome sight she's ever seen. Tucking her hand comfortably in his, she says, "Let's go home," and a small smile of triumph soothes the lines from her face.

Simon smiles back slowly, understanding why she ignores the glow Charity leaves in his eyes. "I love you, Mary," he says.

And the sound of cymbals soars through his veins, enriching him with Charity's gifts: the gift of life, the gift of wisdom and the gift of love.

Autumn Tears

As my time comes nearer, I'm afraid, more afraid than I've ever been in my short life.

"Tree," I ask, "can't you keep me?"

"You must go," the tree says.

"Why? One leaf more or fewer won't make any difference to Earth."

Tree shakes his head sternly. "It is written in your stars that you, to be the very best you can be, must fall. As fall we all must, when our time has come."

"You are eight hundred years old, Tree, and still you stand."

"Leaf," his voice is sad and gentle, "you cannot ever be anything but a leaf. You can be a great leaf, or a small leaf. It is how you fall that will decide your fate. But fall you must: for your good, for the good of us all."

"But you're so perfect, Tree. Everyone remembers you. They admire you, and see God in you, because you live on and on. Why can't I be like you? Why must my life as a leaf be so short and uneventful?"

"Because you are a leaf and I am a tree. One day my time will come, and then I, too, will fall."

His words make sense in my head. Yet my heart still trembles in fear as I think of the day I must die.

Too soon, the days become cooler; my skin turns from verdant green to pale yellow and, finally, a rich, red russet.

"Goodbye, Leaf," Tree says, bending in the autumn wind. "I'll miss you." Softly he shakes his branches.

A mighty roar rends the air as my stem tears away from the safety of Tree's bark. I'm all on my own, falling ... falling ... falling ... screaming out my pain and terror.

Ever downwards I twirl, brushing against a calloused lichen, its ochre face hardened by struggle.

"Watch it, Leaf," she snaps. "We don't all have it so easy in life."

Easy? She thought this was easy? To surrender; to give up all I am, to become I know not what. Until, oh, slowly, so slowly, I learn how beautiful it is. How at peace I find myself, floating feather-soft on every breath of air. I land on a patch of moss, admiring how my autumn coat contrasts so strikingly with the spongy carpet.

Then I gasp my last sigh and realise how right Tree is: all is as it is, as it is meant to be.

The Sullen Bell

Where I land, it is dark, dark and lonely. In the distance, I hear the faint cries of those who were with me when the old tunnel collapsed, but it's impossible to see even the tips of my fingers.

Cautiously, I move: first, my legs, and then my arms. Despite the ferocity of the falling rocks, I am—incredibly—unharmed. But for a few bruises, I'm the same as when I stepped into the cage this morning to begin my shift.

The gully is small and cramped. I have to manoeuvre myself onto my stomach in stages. My headlamp is broken, but it's a blessing for, when I turn my head to the east, there is a lessening of the night thickness, a glimmer that beckons.

My heart thuds with relief. I say a prayer, and another. One prayer of thanks; one a plea for help.

Is this the only way forward for me? If it is, I must leave behind those soft sounds of all I knew before I fell; the comfort of those voices, muffled now by the thick wall of rock and dust that separates me from them.

The air thickens around me, as if there is someone with me, there in the darkness. Knowing I am alone, yet I hope.

"Hello? Is anyone there … *there* … *there*?" I call out.

In the heavy silence that follows the dying echo of my voice, I find the courage to drag myself forward; away from the security of the other side and towards the unknown light.

As I get closer, I hear a bell begin to sound; it rings and rings, a surly imperative telling me I can't wait for those voices any more, for the rocks above are groaning and creaking with whispers of danger. The dust has hardly settled from the first rockfall and already another threatens. It chokes me now, drying my throat. I want to tell them to hurry, hurry, for time is vanishing.

Instead, I leave the small hollow that has become a womb, safe and dark and comfortable. I can't go back to them, no matter how desperately I want to cling to the thuds and clinks of impending rescue.

Millimetre by excruciating millimetre, I drag myself through the narrowing crevasse, the ringing bell my guide in the darkness. My hard-hat, then my boots, and finally my overall, all must go, if I am to avoid being trapped in this fissure.

There are signs of old life here; men have trodden this way before. The dim shape of an old water bottle. Another discarded miner's hat. Both give me hope as the air gets fresher and the darkness lightens until, in an unexpected rush, the ground dips sharply downward and, as the ringing bell stops abruptly, I spill into a cave.

Small and eerie, there is the slow, steady plop of mineral-laden water as it drips off the stalactites: fingers of an unseen God, pointing downward to the life-giving water of an underground lake, upon which bobs an old tattered raft. Loosely tied to a rusted iron bolt, it is a way out.

At first reluctant to trust my life to such a flimsy ride, I crawl around the water's edge. Except for the steep slope that leads up to where I've come from—far steeper from this angle than I had thought when I plunged down—there is only the small patch of ground I stand on, a natural jetty jutting out of the seeping rock and leading to the raft.

There is no other way to escape but across this vast expanse of water.

The raft is thin and damp and mouldy from years of neglect. It's also surprisingly stable as I clamber aboard and release the rusted chain from the bolt. My hands are my paddles and, just as I tire, an undertow, invisible under the dark mirror surface of the lake, takes the raft. I lie back, uncaring of the faint dampness that seeps through my naked skin as I leave all the worry, all the fear, behind me.

I have done what I must; all that is left is to watch as the raft drifts into the approaching light, whiter and brighter than any I have seen before. Closer it comes as the raft swirls faster and faster until the light surrounds me and, with a final rush, I leave the darkness behind and tumble into another world.

Love Token

"Give me a token," I say.

"Why?"

"So that I know you mean what you say."

Her arms spread wide at her sides as bewilderment turns her eyes from moss to dank earth. "Don't you trust me?"

I shrug. What can one say to a blunt question like that? If I'm honest, will it bring back the smile she once had?

"I don't trust anyone any more."

She's silent. I say nothing, taking my pleasure from looking over the soft fall of brown curls, the flutter of her hands, as she tries to make sense of what I'm asking.

How did we reach this point? I grimace. It was inevitable. From the day I was born, this moment was inevitable.

Despite it all, I can't bear to see her discomfort.

"You shouldn't be surprised," I say.

"I'm not. You'll always hate me."

I shake my head. "I'll always love you."

"Then why don't you trust me?"

"How can I? *You* walked out on us."

A sigh. Some more hand flutters. Then she jumps up and walks to stare out the window.

"I came back," she says, but doesn't turn to meet my accusing eyes. "Doesn't that count for anything?"

"It should," I agree. "But the risk is always there."

That makes her face me. "There *is* no risk! Not any more."

"How do I know?" And I smile slightly as frustration crimps her lips closed, scouring the wrinkles next to her mouth deeper than before.

"Because I've promised you, and your father, that I'll never leave again."

"I'm your son," I remind her. "You forgot that when you left with your lover."

A guilty glare, but then she's back, fighting. "You don't know everything! The reasons ... you're only fourteen!"

"So tell me what I don't know," and the power surges through me as I see her considering my demand.

"I was lonely ... your father ..." She swipes a hand over her eyes, doubting the rightness of this.

I wait, showing no mercy. "My father ...?" I prompt, when she shows no signs of going on.

"He was always away on business. I had no one to talk to."

"You had me."

"You're my child. How could I make my problems yours?"

I'm implacable, merciless, in my response to that. "You did, in the end. When you left us."

"Don't be like that," she cries. "I love you! I'll never leave you again!"

"Give me a token," I say.

She slumps back into the soft velvet couch, her tears a balm to my still-bleeding heart.

The Lottery Ticket

The buxom centrefold from *Drum* magazine, staring back at him. A decades-old article 'Time to get the Colour Monkey off your Back.' Once, he'd found it inspiring. Next to that, the fading photo of Nelson Mandela, his hand raised in triumph as he left Pollsmoor Prison.

All unchanged. All still peeling off the walls of his shack.

Patrick Dlamini groaned as he sat up on the side of his bed and lowered his bare feet onto the plastic sheet he'd spread across the damp floor.

It must have rained again in Diepsloot, he thought, wiggling his toes in the icy water before stretching to ease the kinks out of his back. His head felt twice its size again and his knuckles were raw with pain. The older he got, the less homebrew he could drink in a night at the shebeen, and the harder Cebile's head became as he taught her the proper way to respect a husband.

Sighing, knowing there was no other way to start the day, he stood up and winced as he sank ankle-deep into the water, drenching the hems of his pyjamas, so old and worn they—like Patrick's heart—had no warmth left in the weave of their fabric.

But Patrick remembered what his mother had said to him all those years ago when he'd left his village, deep in the foothills of the great Drakensberg Mountains.

"Never forget who you are, Patrick," she'd said, soon after he'd finished school and was leaving home for Johannesburg where, they said, a willing man could find work. Her small hands, their joints already twisting with arthritis although she wasn't even forty yet, worked slowly, packing some stiff *iPhutu* and meat in his scoff tin, so that he wouldn't go hungry on the long road up north. "You are my son, my first-born. I have taught you how to be a man: respect your elders, work hard and always wear pyjamas. Important men always wear pyjamas."

That was thirty-five years ago and he'd only been back to Bonjaneni twice. Once to find a wife, a good woman to bring him comfort and give him many fine sons and, ten years later, to bury his mother.

As he'd watched them slaughter the cow he couldn't afford, but had to buy, and later helped bury her coffin under the heavy red soil, he'd wondered if she knew how badly he'd failed her. For, in the great city of the north, he was not alone in looking for a way to make his dreams come true. Millions, just like him, flocked to the city of gold, where the mud and the dirt and the violence of the shantytowns, growing like rank and poisonous mushrooms on the outskirts of the towering concrete city, could too easily crush a man's hope.

Every night he still wore pyjamas to bed.

Sometimes, when he wasn't too tired or too hungry, he wished they made him feel like the man that his mother had wanted him to be.

There was no respect here. No work either, except on the odd, lucky occasion when, standing in the parking lot outside Builders Warehouse with a hundred other starving men, someone picked his face from the crowd and gave him a job for an hour, or a day or, like the miracle that had happened yesterday, a job for the week.

So happy with the unexpected work that, when he'd received his day's wages, Patrick remembered the grumbles of those unlucky men and decided to buy a lottery ticket at the corner café. Under the bright red name was a painting of a big white woman, with blonde hair, smiling blue eyes and the body of a woman who could give a man many fine sons.

She'd looked just like her picture on the wall and, as she handed over the lottery ticket, she'd boomed. "Good luck, my friend. Maybe today's your lucky day," and she handed him an old *vetkoek*, filled with leftover gravy.

When he'd reached the sprawling edges of Diepsloot, he'd been so thirsty after the long day's work, and the heat and sweat of fifteen bodies crushed into a taxi, he'd been unable to resist entering Shamiso's Shebeen and buying a jug of *mbamba*.

Cebile, as usual, had whined about both the homebrew and the lotto ticket last night when he'd staggered in around midnight. He'd shut her up in the easiest way he knew.

His wife, he thought, wasn't half the woman his mother had been.

Abruptly turning back to the bed, he looked at Cebile sleeping pressed against the corrugated iron wall, shivering with her dreams, or with the cold he'd let in when he'd flung the threadbare orange blanket back.

"Wake up," he shouted. "I need food. I've got work today."

"If you weren't so lazy, you'd have work every day," she muttered.

Perhaps it was only the echo of her words from last night that he heard for, when he leaned across the narrow space to grab her shoulder, wincing as his bruised hands made contact with the cold tin wall, her eyes were still screwed tightly shut. He ignored the swollen cheek with its deep purple bruise as he dragged her off the bed. His lip curled as he saw the pathetic figure of a woman she made, all skin and bone, her breasts—once so large and full of the promise of suckling strong, healthy sons—shrunken and so small they barely pressed against her thin cotton nightgown. Like his pyjamas, they were some other woman's cast-offs, a woman who even now probably lay wrapped in a warm bed, with an electric blanket, never having known a day's bitter cold in her life. And, as Cebile fell with a thud into the water that still numbed his feet, he kicked her.

"Patrick!" she cried, her hands instinctively flying across her face in a protective gesture. He ignored it, as he ignored the blood that had seeped from the crusty scab on her lip during the night and had trickled in an erratic path to her ear before drying up and hardening, just like those useless, dangling breasts that had never given him the sons he wanted.

"Get up," he said, and used his foot to push her towards the small primus stove in the corner of the room. "Cook me some porridge. If I can work hard, maybe I'll keep the job next week." He gave her another shove, so that she began crawling like an awkward river crab across the floor.

Patrick picked up the trousers he'd discarded in the dark and clicked his tongue. She didn't even keep his clothes clean. But these were the only work clothes he had, so he sat back on the bed and shrugged himself into the trousers, holding his feet off the floor. As he wriggled and twisted, the jingling of coins reminded him.

"My lotto ticket!" he cried, frantically patting his pockets until he heard a comforting crackle of paper in the pocket of his shirt.

"Yesterday was my lucky day," he boasted. "I'm the only one who got a job *and* a free *vetkoek*." He waved the lotto ticket under his nose, sniffing deeply. "Mmm ... muh. This is the smell of a lucky ticket."

"You always say that," Cebile grumbled. "But you never win."

"I won last week."

"R70."

"Enough to buy *iPhutu* for a month," he reminded her.

"But not enough to pay the rent."

"*Yooh.*" he said, "You ungrateful woman. You—you with your prayers to the ancestors and to the white man's God. What good does that do you?" He swept the scoff tin she'd been wiping out of her hands and it clattered loudly against the wall of the shack. "What good does that do anyone?" He shoved the lotto ticket back into his pocket and spat on the ground. "Look around you—people die here. Every day. Every hour. People who are no longer people but animals. All we have to live for is to die quickly."

"Your breakfast," Cebile cried after him as he stormed towards the door, a thick sheet of green plastic slapping noisily against the tin walls because he'd forgotten to tie it down last night. "You can't work hungry."

He ignored her and didn't stop walking until he reached the taxi rank. He picked through the meagre supply of coins still left in his pocket, but there wasn't enough to buy food, not even a week-old apple, as well as pay his taxi fare for the day. He looked hungrily at the collection of fruits, nuts and packets of Cheese Crisps spread out on a wooden plank, braced across a couple of half-broken bricks.

"Hey, sister," he said to the young woman behind the counter, trying to smile the smile his mother had said could charm a bird out of a tree. "I'm off to work. Tonight I'll have cash—plenty cash. How about you lend me an apple until then?"

The woman, dressed warmly against the cold in a funny pink woollen hat with knitted braids hanging down over the ears, and an old tracksuit top tucked into a bright blue sarong, just laughed at him.

Cursing her and his empty stomach, he clambered into the battered taxi, already filling up with people anxious to get to work. Fingering the crumpled lotto ticket in his pocket, he hoped his luck from yesterday held. Perhaps he'd win enough to buy food and, if he were very lucky, he'd win enough to pay the rent too. And, if he didn't win, maybe the woman from the café would give him another stale *vetkoek.* Today, she might even fill it with steaming mince and tomato, or add some lamb stew to the thick gravy she'd given him last night … the saliva poured into his mouth.

"*ukuHamba!*" He urged the taxi driver to get moving. Roodepoort was a long way from Diepsloot and, at this time of the morning, the Eastern Bypass always had traffic jams, delaying transport for hours. But a man took work where he could find it. When he found it.

The taxi squealed to a stop in front of the café, speeding off to deliver his next passenger, even before Patrick's feet had hit the pavement. As early as it still was, the blonde woman was there, rolling up the heavy security grille with an ease that told of her strength.

"*Môre,* my friend," she greeted, and laughed, even though there was nothing to laugh at. "You're early today."

Patrick, his heart beating faster, his mouth as dry as it had been wet with saliva earlier, was drawn to her with a desire so secret, so impossible, he could barely remember the night dreams he'd had about this large *white* woman, who had breasts bountiful enough to feed six sons, and a body strong enough to care for them.

"*Sanibonani*, Mama," he mumbled, only just stopping himself from calling her 'Madam', because, even though he'd been born into a country unshackling itself from its colonial masters, even though he'd lived through nearly twenty years of freedom, nothing much changed for you when you were poor.

"Can you check lotto?" he asked, his stomach growling so loudly a rush of shame warmed the blood in his cheeks.

"Do you think today's your lucky day, hey?" she asked.

As she spoke, she ladled some steaming mince into two *vetkoek.* Wrapping them into wax paper, she pushed them across the counter, and said, "It is!" Her laugh filled the empty shop, and Patrick's eyes closed in ecstasy as he bit into the crispy fried dough and fragrant filling, the first taste of meat he'd had in months.

"Yes, Madam, I am lucky today," he said. He didn't care what he called her, because all he could think of was the taste of the meat on his tongue.

"Maybe today's the day you win the big jackpot, hey?" she said, as she took his ticket from him and scanned it.

The lotto machine, with its bright yellow and red logo, remained depressingly silent.

"Sorry, my friend," she said, pushing the ticket back over the counter, its top marked with cigarette burns and scratches from the countless coins that had exchanged hands over its wooden face. "Your luck's run out."

Patrick looked at her blankly. Then her words registered. "So I didn't win today." He shrugged with an acceptance born from too many hopes left unfulfilled. "I'll try again tomorrow." With his stomach full and a job waiting for him, he was lucky enough.

He grinned at her as he picked up the second *vetkoek,* still steaming lazily in its wrapper. "This will feed my wife tonight," he said, although his still hollow stomach made him wonder how he'd stop himself from eating it before he reached home. "Maybe next week I'll get another job to pay the rent."

The woman looked as serious as her round, friendly face allowed, tapping the creased lottery ticket slowly against her lips. "Wait," she said as he turned to leave the shop. "Sometimes this *blerrie* machine plays up. I'll scan the ticket one more time."

She pressed some buttons to clear the machine and then slid the ticket back into the slot.

"*Jislaaik*!' she said as the machine beeped and blinked. She collapsed onto the three-legged stool, its grey plastic cover fraying in the front where her thick thighs rubbed it day after day. "This has never happened before!"

"What, Mama?" Patrick asked, not sure if he should go around the counter to help her because her face was so pale and her hands flapped in front of her like the wings of a chicken he'd once slaughtered back home in the village.

"What's your name, my friend?"

"Patrick." His mother had said a man is not a man unless the person he speaks to knows both his names, so he added, "Patrick Dlamini."

"*Kom hier*, Patrick Dlamini," the woman said, her blue eyes suddenly as bright as a hot summer sky. "Come here behind the counter."

Replacing his spare *vetkoek* carefully on the counter, so the juice didn't leak out too much, Patrick squeezed past her. Squinting at the screen he was grateful that his mother, a schoolteacher before she'd married, had also made him learn to read and write.

CONTACT NATIONAL LOTTERY HEAD OFFICE, he read. CALL 011 555 6214 AT EARLIEST CONVENIENCE.

He looked at her, trying hard not to be aware of her heavy scent in the small, hot space, a scent that made him think terrible thoughts.

"What does it mean?" he asked.

She rocked the stool back on its spindly legs. "It means, Patrick," she said, grinning as she slapped him on the shoulder, "that you are a lucky man. You're a winner."

"I've won?"

"You've won big."

"How much?"

"I can only pay up to R5000," she said and stood up, crowding him out of her space, as she reached into the machine and pulled out the ticket. "Here," she said, taking his hand and folding his nerveless fingers over it. "Keep this safe." She saw he was lost, so she took his hand and helped him tuck the ticket in his shirt pocket. "Go home to your wife. Tomorrow, you take your identity document—the new green one—and go to the address on the back of the ticket. Tell them you've won. Don't give anyone the ticket until you're sure it's the right person. Too many people will steal you blind in this country."

"How much have I won?" he asked again, desperation and hope slurring his words in equal measure.

On the counter, buried beneath a pile of serviettes and the box that held the straws mixed with plastic knives and forks, was a telephone. She dragged it towards her and, pulling a pair of reading glasses out of her bag, dialled the number displayed on the screen of the Lotto machine.

"*Môre*," she said. "This is *Tannie* Marie from Roodepoort, agent 0200853. There's a Lotto customer here—his ticket has won big. The machine says I must call you …"

She took his ticket from him and read the numbers out.

"He's won?" she said eventually.

"How *much*?" he groaned.

"He wants to know how much," she said, and waited. "Okay."

Patrick just looked at the phone she held out to him. "Go on," she said, and shook the instrument. "Take it, it's not a snake."

Pressing the cold plastic against his ear, he listened and listened until he pulled it away from his ear and stared at it as if it *were* a snake. Then, silently, because he couldn't speak a word, he replaced the handset in its cradle.

"That much, hey?" she asked, tucking his ticket back in his pocket.

He nodded, because his lips were as frozen as his mind as it replayed what he had just heard.

"Congratulations," the disembodied voice had said. "Bring your lotto ticket and your proof of identity to our Head Office in Midrand. The rollover jackpot is R5.6 million for the winning ticket."

He was sure that was what the upbeat voice on the phone had said.

Five point six million rand.

Here he stood, with his stomach only half-filled with stale *vetkoek*, wearing cast-off clothes and shoes with no laces, and he was a millionaire?

The hiss of a can of cola opening jerked him out of his trance. "Here," the Afrikaans woman said, not asking how much he'd won. "Drink this, you're in shock." She took a bag, and loaded it with a loaf of bread, some milk and sugar and tea, a few tins of baked beans and the meat-filled *vetkoek.* "Take this to your wife. It might be a while before the money comes through to you. Even lucky men must eat."

He couldn't help it. He clapped his hands together and dipped his knees in the old way of gratitude.

"Ag," she said her cheeks red with the shame of the past. "None of that now. You can come back later and pay me."

Then she led him outside to the pavement and flung up a hand to hail a passing taxi as if she'd spent her life boarding them.

All the way back to Diepsloot, Patrick sat silently. He couldn't talk; he couldn't hear anything but that voice over the phone.

Five point six million rand. Five point six million rand.

He got off at Diepsloot Extension 1 taxi rank and walked past the hawker who'd refused to give him an apple this morning. He walked past the brightly coloured clothes, flapping in the wind and the black-and-white puppy, snapping playfully at its exhausted mother's scraggly tail.

As he stepped over the stream of leaking sewerage that no one ever came to fix to reach his shack, he was beginning to dream. Real dreams, this time, not dreams that melted in the morning as soon as the sun rose.

Come back later, she'd said. *You can come back later*.

When he opened the flap to the shack he shared with Cebile, and saw her back on the narrow bed, her thin unhappy face clenched, her arms crossed against those small, dried-up breasts that had never been able to suckle one of the six babies she'd carried to life, his future lay clear before him.

Dropping the bag of food he carried by the door, he shouted, "Get out of here!" His head buzzing with excitement and his heart thumping louder and louder in his chest, he crossed the room with one bold step. Turning the bed upside down, he tipped his wife and all the blankets onto the still damp floor.

"*uSile wena*! I don't need a useless wife, Cebile. Look," he cried and hauled the precious Lotto ticket out of his pocket where his White Goddess had placed it.

"I'm rich. Rich, I tell you." He waved it under her half-dazed eyes. "Rich enough to buy a new wife. One who will give me sons." He aimed a careless kick at her belly. "I'll be an important man. You can clean my floors, because that's all you're good for. I'll live in a big house with a big wife, whose breasts will suckle my children to life not like you—"

The excitement buzzing in his head, the beauty of his vision of the future overwhelmed him. Abruptly, he sat down on the broken beer crate that was the only chair he had. He put his hand, the one clutching the lotto ticket, over his chest to stop the thundering of his heart from getting any louder.

He'd throw Cebile out when he'd rested. He was in shock, he thought, and closed his eyes, resting his head back against the rusted corrugated iron wall …

Hours later, just before the sun set, when Patrick hadn't moved, or made a single sound, not even the hacking cough that sometimes woke them both when he couldn't stop the phlegm, Cebile crept out from behind the overturned bed. Crawling along the floor in case he woke, she tentatively touched his foot.

"Patrick," she whispered. "Wake up."

He still didn't open his eyes.

Moving slowly, so that the bruises on her back and the pain in her ribs hurt less, she stood up and unwrapped his cold, cold fingers from around the lotto ticket.

He had said this ticket would make him rich. How rich, Cebile, wondered, was rich?

She stood for a long time, her bare feet on the damp plastic sheeting getting colder and colder, as she stared down at the ticket.

Had her prayers been strong enough? Did this small piece of paper carry enough luck to get her home to the village of her ancestors?

That place where people didn't die by the hour and the view beyond her door wasn't row upon row of tumbling down shacks, but of rolling green hills brushed by the wind carrying the voices of village women laughing and chattering as they washed their clothes in the pure clean mountain streams.

Perhaps there would be enough left over after the bus ticket to buy a small plot of land, where she could build a mud hut and buy a cow for fresh milk, and some chickens for eggs and conversation when she was lonely.

She sighed, and tucked the ticket deep into the pocket of her skirt.

Tomorrow would be a new start for her, she thought, but tonight she must still fetch Pastor Eddie from the First Gospel Burial Society. He would lay Patrick out and she would begin to mourn her husband.

Just as a good wife should.

The Blue Mountains

The day I left my childhood behind, I was playing in the mud on the edge of a field of fading yellow sunflowers. The shadows of the mountains fell over me as my mother, her still-pretty face tense with worry, ran up to me. My father, his narrow forehead decorated in the elaborate blue-and-white beaded band that told of his chiefdom, followed more sedately.

"Wife," he said, resting a hand on my mother's shoulder. The nail of his right forefinger twisted crookedly from the time when, as a child my age, he'd struggled to free a lost calf. A rock, loose and heavy in the red soil that covered so much of the barren heights of the Blue Mountains, fell and crushed his finger, forever marking the nail. "You knew when you married me this time would come."

My mother, her hands twisting into her stomach as if that way she could stop her wrenching tears, only wailed. "She's just a baby!"

"Chiamaka is six years old. No younger than I was."

"But she's a *girl*!" Another wail escaped her, this one so deep her breasts, still sumptuous after suckling seven children, jiggled. "You have your sons."

"The law of the ancestors says '*all the chief's children*.'" My father's face was tight; he loved her so much he had only taken one wife. His reward was the seven children my mother bore him, all healthy and all living. I was the youngest, and the only daughter. He didn't want to hurt her, but his dark gaze was implacable as it rested on me, naked but for the red ooze of mud clinging to my skin as I sat in the puddle that was to become the final playground of my childhood.

"She should be learning how to grind the corn and make *iPhutu pap*. She should be learning how to braid hair and care for children … don't you want grandchildren?" Her emotion overwhelming her, my mother—for the first time in my life—dropped to her knees, as she should do when supplicating a chief such as my father. Although it was his right, as Chief of the Luvenda, he, in his wisdom and his love, had never demanded this usual sign of submission from her.

"Stop your wailing, wife." He shook her hands free from their hold on the strip of leopard skin that crossed under his chin, across the lean planes of his chest until it tucked into his loincloth decorated with the same blue-and-white symbols as his headband. "Chiamaka may not be The One." His voice was stern enough to silence my mother but, with her head lowered to the sand, she could not see what I saw: the glitter of moisture adding a sheen to his brown eyes that turned them as blue as the distant mountains.

I knew then that he knew I *was* The One. In the heavy swirl of excitement that engulfed me, I started to hiccup and, with each *hic*, I felt myself growing a little taller as I stood up from the puddle of mud and waited for my destiny.

"Come, daughter," my father said, holding out his broad hand, with its strong spatula fingers that always made me feel so safe. "This time you will come to the *khoro*. Your brothers are already waiting."

My hiccups stopped: born ten years after the youngest of my father's six sons, and a girl as well, I wasn't close to any of them for they saw me as a child. But to be included in the village council meeting must mean I was fully grown now. I stood up, ineffectually wiping the mud from body until my mother, silent still since my father's order, plucked some green sunflower leaves and, with a few strategic wipes, had me as clean as I could ever be without immersing myself in the river that watered our land.

Soon, we arrived at the ancient baobab tree, where my brothers, and all the people of the village, milled around its huge trunk as they waited for the *khoro* to begin. Red dust puffed in small clouds around the hundreds of bare feet tramping the hallowed ground, made smooth as a river washed stone by the many gatherings that had come before this one. For, the legends said, this tree had stood for ten thousand years providing our people with food, medicine and shelter.

Despite the lowing of a large herd of cattle held back by a few roughly stripped acacia tree branches, there was an unearthly silence hanging over the waiting people: the silence of breath held as one waited for the assegai to fly from the hand of a warrior. Only the occasional squawk of a baby—disturbed from its slumber as its mother dropped to her knees before the Chief, my father, walking past her on the path opening through the crowd—broke the still air.

In front of the gnarled old trunk stood my brothers, from the eldest at nearly thirty summers, to the youngest, but ten years older than I, murmuring to the *Makhadzi*, the old woman who, when our people were sick, spoke to our ancestors to heal our spirits and gave us herbs to heal our bodies.

As was customary, my mother stopped as we reached the edge of the low-hanging branches, spreading out from the heavy trunk like the arms of a mother protecting her family. I held her hand tightly, too scared to tell her to stop crying; that the patter of excitement running through my veins as softly as a mouse ran through the grass roof of our hut in the shadows of the night was nothing to cry about.

My father, realising I was no longer at his side, turned to me. "Come, Chia," he said, and the sadness was back in his eyes, but pride was there too, and a quiet encouragement.

"She can't come into the circle," my third oldest brother snarled. "She's a girl!" My other brothers, brave now another had spoken, grumbled their agreement.

"Chia is here for the same reason you are," my father said, "because I have called for her presence."

My brother dropped his gaze first.

Then the *Makhadzi*, her rough cloth skirt woven in the colours of the autumn trees and swirling in a gust of hot wind, stepped forward, raising the bent wooden stick she carried to the sky.

"The time is now," she said. In descending height, she lined up all seven of my father's children beside him. She handed him his cow-skin shield and assegai and threw his leopard skin cloak around his shoulders, attaching a crown of antelope skin to his beaded headband, with two large ostrich feathers that bobbed and weaved with each movement he made.

She scraped twigs and dried branches together and set them alight. She began chanting, at first softly, then louder and louder as the twigs smouldered and, when the first flame leapt from the crackling mound, she scattered herbs into the fire: rosemary for clarity and the sacred *imphepo* herb to call to the spirits of our ancestors.

The smell and the smoke made my head spin and my heart beat faster and faster as she started beating her drum in time with her chants until my father held up his assegai and she abruptly fell silent.

As the smoke of the sacred herbs swirled in the silence around us, my father began to speak.

"My people, one day I will no longer be Chief." Cries broke from the throats of the villagers, for he was a much-loved leader, but he stilled them by holding up his assegai. "The way of nature is that from the Earth we have come and to her we all must return."

He dropped the point of his spear to the ground, flicking up a scattering of dust that fell from its tip, glinting in the sun, as he continued, "The laws of the tribe and of the tribal ancestors will choose my successor as your Chief."

"When my ancestors came to me in the night, visiting my dreams and whispering into my heart, they told me the time had come to begin the training of the next leader of our people." He pointed at his cattle, unsettled and restless from the chanting and the smoke, and said, "I will divide my cattle into seven herds: you, my children, will each care for a herd for one full cycle of the moon. You will take food and, two days hence, when the moon is full and pale, you will each drive your herd into foothills of the Blue Mountains."

His first son, my oldest brother, would go in the direction of the Dragon's Back, he said; his second son towards the Dragon's Spear and so on, until he came to me.

"And you, Chia, you will take the seventh herd into the Valley of the Pregnant Woman."

My brothers shuffled and shifted with unease and looked at me, then at each other, with sullen eyes, but no one, not even Kofi, my third-oldest brother and the strongest, dared interrupt him.

"My successor as Chief of the Luvenda people will be chosen by this method," he continued. "You will each care for your herd and, when the moon has gorged the sky empty of stars and is full of light again, you will bring my cattle back to me."

He looked us over, one by one. "*All* of my cattle," he said, "For if you cannot look after the beasts in the field, how can you look after your people?"

#

As we left the village, my excitement was as strong as my fear. This was the most responsibility I'd ever had: were my brothers' whispers true?

"A girl has no place in the line of Chiefs!" Kofi had complained.

"Let him give her a herd, she's only a girl," they'd all laughed. I'd glared at them, but they only laughed again. "She's too young and, surely, as the sun rises each morning, she'll kill all the cattle—or herself—long before the stars disappear into the belly of the moon again."

My father had insisted and so I, too, left with my bundle of food. With more running than I had ever done before, and using the same crooning noises my mother had sung to calm me as a baby when the fierce storms raged over the kraals, I drove the unruly cattle ahead of me with a stick.

The days that followed were hard and hot, and the nights cold and long, but I learnt how to calm the animals when the growl of a hungry leopard echoed across the valley hidden beneath the towering mountains. I learnt how to care for them as if they were the children I would one day have, and I even learnt how to birth a new calf, for within the first few days I realised one of the cows was pregnant.

When her time came, in the middle of one of the storms I dreaded so much, she lowed and lowed with pain. Praying to the ancestors of my people for help and, as I'd seen the *Makhadzi* do from time to time with the wailing women of the village, I pushed my hand up the cow's tunnel of life and, cupping the calf's nose, gently twisted it around until it slipped into the world in a watery rush.

The next morning it was gone from the small kraal I'd built from scraps of wood I'd found near the cave I was sleeping in. After hours of searching, of following its bawls until I found it in an underground cave, sparkling with the tears of the gods that had dripped through the earth above and settled into the darkness of the pool below where my lost calf calmly stood drinking its fill. Its soft brown coat glistened in the light bouncing off the glittering rocks as the sun, rising to its peak, shone into the cave through a slender crack. I whirled round and round until, exhausted from my exhilaration, I fell on my knees next to the calf and drank gratefully from the pool before leading it back to the herd, caged in the rough kraal I had made.

By the time the moon was full again, I knew each of the cattle by the different markings on their coats, and each of them had a name.

I was disinclined to rush back to the village and become a mere girl again, playing in the mud pools or helping grind the corn, but eventually I arrived back in the village, driving my herd ahead of me.

My mother was wailing; my father pacing and Kofi, his third son, gloating: until my arrival, he was the only one who had returned with exactly the same number of cattle as he'd had when he left.

"You're back," my father said. He gave a small cough, clearing his throat as he gripped my shoulder hard, even as my mother fell on her knees examining every part of me for injury or harm.

"Of course," I said as I shrugged off my mother's attentions, for she was fussing over the child I no longer was.

His laugh boomed out like a crack of thunder and his grip tightened for an instant, before he turned to count the cattle I had herded into the village. He counted the last head and turned to look at me.

"You're a good girl," he praised, "and you'll make a fine Chief on the day I return to the fields of our ancestors."

Chaos erupted.

"*I'm* your successor!" Kofi said, balling his hand so tightly the skin looked thin and smooth. "I am your son! I am older than Chia!" With each sentence, he banged his fist into his chest, and then shook it at his herd. "And I, too, brought back all my cattle!"

The Chief, our father, was unmoved. "So you did," he said. "Didn't you?" He pointed his flywhisk at my brother's herd, and the snail shells and black feathers of the fish eagle on its handle twirled slyly. "Do you know their names yet?"

"Names? What names?" Kofi frowned. "Cattle don't have names."

My father turned to me. "Chiamaka, do *your* cattle have names?"

I nodded.

"What is the calf called?" He pointed to the young calf I had helped birth. She'd become my favourite and, as I rubbed her silky head, she mooed and tried to lick me.

"Glittering Tear."

As my brothers, led by my third brother Kofi, guffawed, my father ignored them. A smile touched his lips, such a small smile I couldn't even see the missing tooth at the back of his mouth, which only showed when he laughed loudly. He nodded. "Where did you get her name?"

I dropped my chin, avoiding his eyes, for I realised I'd have to tell him how close I'd come to losing one of my herd. "Come, child." I shivered as the coarse horsetail of his flywhisk scratched my chin as he used it to lift my gaze to his. "Tell us how you found that name."

My voice faltering at times, so that he had to ask me to repeat myself, I told how I'd almost lost the calf, not once, at her birth, but twice, when she escaped to the cave of the glittering tears.

But, "That is a good name, Chia," was all he said when I finished my tale. Then he asked me, "Have you named every one of these beasts that depend on you? Even the oldest? The weakest?"

"I know every name of every beast in my herd," I said, my chin tilting up, even though I knew I should not be so proud of such a simple task. "That one is Granny, because she is so old," I said, "and that brown one, with the white patch, is White Eye and—"

His full lips held onto his smile, and his eyes half-closed as he interrupted me to ask my brother, "Do you see, Kofi? Chia even named the old cattle, while you could not name one of the animals in your herd."

"I was too busy to give the dumb animals names," sneered my brother, as he wiped away a drop of sweat rolling down his cheek, even though the sun was starting to slide behind the *khoro* tree, bringing a welcome relief from the heat.

My father's flywhisk stopped its steady *whishwhishwhish.* "Come here," he ordered.

Kofi sauntered up to us, his loincloth, hitched low under his belly fat, swirling around his knees and the rattles attached to the strips of impala pelts around his ankles jingling with each confident step.

My father held up his finger, the one crushed long ago, and said, "Tell me again, third son of mine, why, when the sun sets on this day, you should be named my successor as Chief?"

"I am a man." He thumped his bare chest, already thick with fat for the whole village knew Kofi liked more than his share as we ate in the shade of the *boma*. "I am older than Chia." Encouraged by the rising mutters of the listening villagers, he continued, "And, while my first brother lost ten cattle and my fourth brother lost his whole herd, I—" he paused triumphantly, his bare feet spread wide apart in the dust to balance his weight as his chest swelled out like an old brown river toad calling to its mate, "—I brought back every beast I left with."

"*All* your herd?" my father asked, that small smile still tugging at the corner of his mouth. "Did you really?"

"Did I what?"

"Bring back every beast you left with?"

"Yes!"

My father said nothing, and all the villagers fell silent until the only noise was the flywhisk moving back and forth, back and forth, with the occasional dart and slap that killed an errant fly with deceptive ease.

Kofi glared at me, then at my father. "Except for the calf!" he shouted. "One of the cows was pregnant! She gave birth to a girl-calf, but it wandered off and I couldn't find it. It bawled for days," he snarled. "But I couldn't find it."

"And yet Chia—she who is the youngest of you all, and a girl, and for these reasons you say she is unworthy to be Chief—she found her calf, and brought it back safely with all the rest of her herd."

He stood up and called the *Makhadzi*. Together they came and stood with me, one on either side.

"My people," my father said. "Never before has it come to pass that our people have had a woman as Chief. But the gods and the ancestors have spoken! One day, when I return to the dust of this land, which has sustained our forefathers for generations, Chiamaka will be your Chief." The crowd hissed and muttered, but he ignored them. "She will be your light and your leader, and you will honour her as you honour me." He pulled himself taller and glared the rising noise into silence. "Or the mountains will no longer thunder, the river will dry up and our people will become strangers to each other."

For a long time, no one moved. Afraid of the silence, which made the air feel like the moments before the storms that rolled off the mountains and thundered around us, I scrabbled for his hand. He did not say a word and the silence grew until my mother dropped to her knees.

"The gods have spoken," she cried. "Chiamaka will be Chief."

Slowly, then in greater numbers, the crowd fell to their knees until only my brothers stood before us. Still my father did not speak and, as I looked up at his face, I saw from the muscles clenching along his jaw, that his quietness was not that of calm, but of a strong man mastering his anger so that it did not tear asunder that which he loved the most: his people.

Whishwhishwhish went his flywhisk until, on almost a sigh, they gave up their struggle against his greater strength and, one by one, with Kofi last to surrender, they sank to their knees to acknowledge the line of chiefs that was to endure through me.

#

That same night, the *Makhadzi* took me high into the Blue Mountains to learn the ways of Chief of the Luvenda, leaving her great niece to take her place as soothsayer of the village.

We passed the muddy sunflower field where I had said goodbye to my childhood; we walked through the green foothills, up into the dense sacred forests of tree ferns and fever trees, and then we crossed into the barrenness of the snow-capped mountaintops.

There were stretches of grey slate, with a few stubby bushes to break the dullness. As we trudged on and on, the air became thin and cold even in the heat of summer. Between my gasps for breath, I pointed to a few stubborn patches of snow.

"That snow is the gift of our ancestors," said the old woman, who was hardly puffing after the long climb with our supplies. "It keeps the rivers in the valley trickling even in the worst of the droughts, just enough to save our people."

A gnarled hand on my arm stopped me. "Look," she said, pointing downwards with her knobkerrie, the tip of the gnarled wooden stick rubbed smooth and round by her hand.

Far below was the village. Tiny round huts, with their roofs of grass and walls of mud, scattered inside the stone walls; people like ants scurrying around; and the White River that had run through the centre of the village for as long as my people had existed.

"We have not known drought for generations, not since your grandfather's grandfather took the throne," the old woman said. "Your lineage is a noble one. Can you learn what that means?"

A stern thread wove through her voice; her eyes, when I looked up into that wrinkled face, were as old the mountains themselves. Something moved inside me, waking to answer the question.

As tired as I was, I pulled myself straighter, drawing on the strength I knew my father would want me to have. "I will learn," I promised.

Her eyes, small as brown berries dried out from being in the sun too long, became smaller as she smiled and walked on until, where the narrow path that led us up the mountain became almost impossible to pass, we turned a corner and found an old hut.

The stone walls stood strong, although they bore the scars of the fire that had destroyed the roof and blackened the door and walls.

"What happened?" I asked.

"The finger of the gods," the old woman said, "knows the right time to strike." As if hearing her, far in the belly of the mountains there was a faint flash, followed by the rumble of thunder.

I shivered and asked, "Who lives here?"

"The future Chiefs of our people live here," she said, and dropped her heavy sack to the ground, stretching as far as her bent old bones would allow. "We will live here. Fetch those stones." She pointed to the pieces of slate piled beneath a jagged ledge. "We begin again."

Half frozen with cold, for the day had begun to slip into the shadows of the night, and half frozen with fear of the future, I rubbed my hands together to stop their shaking. "*Makhadzi*, how long are we to rest here?"

"Until you are ready to lead your people."

"How long will that take?"

"Questions, child, so many questions!" She sighed, and answered me anyway. "The mountains will tell us when you are ready."

Only my stomach growled in reply. Ashamed, hoping she had not heard the sound, I looked around at the land, which looked even more unfriendly as the night began to swallow it up and I whispered, "What if our supplies run out? How will we eat?"

"What your father does not leave underneath the Baboon Rock each full moon, the mountains will provide."

#

So it was.

The rains came and the rains went for many seasons. Even as my body changed from a girl's into a woman's, the mountains taught me what the *Makhadzi* did not. I grew used to the crack of thunder and the flash of light that told us the gods were still pleased with our people.

I watched the grounds for signs of drought.

"As chief, you must bring the rains to both the land and the spirits of the people," the *Makhadzi* said. "When the land is dusty and dry, our people are starving their souls and so the ancestors starve their bellies to make them remember. You must make them remember, even if it is painful."

I scanned the horizon for the changing colours and the flights of the birds, all clues as to when the rain would come rolling off the mountains. "Remember what?" I asked, looking down at her, for as I had become taller, she had shrunk with age.

"Remember the source of their abundance." She leaned a little heavier on her stick and sighed. "Too often, the people only remember the gods in times of drought." She smiled sadly, her head, with its thin grey hair nearly white now, bobbing up and down. "In times when the corn is plenty and the animals are fat, they forget too easily. It's then you will need to call down the power of the gods. Come," she said, "I will show you how to make the mountains cry the tears of the gods."

But I never could learn how to make rain roll off the mountains into the valley below as she did. Soon, she was too old to make the heavens weep and the land got drier and drier.

One morning, after the moon had hung full and heavy in the dark sky, so close to the earth I could have touched it had I been taller, I woke to found her curled still and serene. Her cow skin was wrapped tightly around her and all I had to do through my tears was to scratch a shallow grave beneath the cold grey shale that surrounded our hut.

Before the next full moon, I walked halfway down the mountain and waited at the Baboon Rock for the one who brought our supplies from the village.

"The *Makhadzi* is dead," I said, when the son of my brother's wife's uncle arrived. "Tell my father I am ready to come home to the village."

At the next full moon, the answer was the same as it was for another hundred moons:

"The Chief says you still have much to learn and must not come home."

He was right. I still had much to learn.

The mountains grew silent and dry as I struggled to learn how to make the rains come.

Even the snows of the winters were thinner, their melt sinking through the cracks in the blue slate peaks long before the water could gorge the river in the valley that had saved our people for generations.

One moon, when I went to Baboon Rock, there were no supplies, not then and not for two more full moons. I dared not leave the mountain until my father gave his permission. I survived by eating tadpoles breeding in the muddy pools that remained trapped between the cracks and crevices. Occasionally I caught a frog, or a lizard, but I grew weaker and scared until the only thunder I heard was that of my rumbling stomach.

It was a cold night, too late for the rains to come, when my father came to me.

"Chiamaka," he said. "Return to the village of the Luvenda. Return to your home."

Although it had been years since I heard him speak, the lilt of his voice was no different from when, as a young girl, I played in the sunflower field; the stroke of his calloused hand on my cheek as gentle as ever.

"I'm not ready," I cried. "I cannot make the mountains weep."

"You must return," he said, withdrawing his hand from my cheek, but when I clutched at his fingers to hold him close, I woke, crying.

In the morning, I gathered my few belongings. The old *Makhadzi*'s knobkerrie, unused since she had last tried to teach me how to make rain, lay on the floor in the hut. I picked it up, thinking it would help me keep my footing as I descended the steeper parts of the mountains. Besides, when I held it, I could hear the echo of her voice teaching me the sacred rain chants.

Delaying the moment of my departure, for, truly, I was not ready to leave this place, I playfully shook the stick at the heavens.

With swift ferocity, the mountains answered me. A jagged bolt of lightning flew from the sky, setting ablaze the hut that had been my home for more moons than I cared to remember, until only the stone walls still stood, as scorched and scarred as when first I had seen them.

The hut was gone, but I still had the old woman's rain stick. I could delay no longer, and so my slow trek out of the mountains began. As I passed Baboon Rock, my fear bubbled over into excitement.

In my dreams, my father had not changed.

In life, would he be bent and grey? Would my mother still be pretty? Who of the friends of my youth had married, had children of their own?

But, as I descended from the desolate peaks, my fear returned. For, instead of lush forests and fields of ripe maize and yellow sunflowers, the closer I came to the village, the more desolate the land became.

In the village, people lay drooped across the doorways of their huts, or leaned lethargically against trees shrivelled by drought and on the edge of dying. Starving dogs, their ribs showing through matted hair, did no more than bare their teeth at me, after so many years away a stranger in my own village.

"*Aa!*" I greeted the people, old and young, but at the hunger and hopelessness in their faces, I could not add a smile to my greeting.

What had my father done to so anger the gods and bring this terrible drought on them?

Or was it I who had failed my people, with my inability to bring the rain as the old *Makhadzi* had tried to teach me?

The sound of shouting, interspersed with a pleading voice I recognised as my mother's, drew me, stumbling, down the path to the *khoro* tree. My mother was on her knees, hands stretched palms upward, her head bowed before the Chief.

But the Chief was not my father … it was Kofi. Dressed in the leopard pelt and blue-beaded headband of the Chief of the Luvenda people, he pushed past my mother to where two of my other brothers held Demba, the last but I of my father's children.

With a vicious swipe, Kofi struck my father's flywhisk across Demba's face and shoulders with such force my mother jumped to her feet to scurry around the edge of them, alternately wringing her hands and covering her face as she cried out for her sons to stop their squabbles.

"I am your Chief." Kofi screeched, his spittle mixing with the blood on Demba's face. "You will obey me. Chia stays where she belongs … in the wastes of the accursed Blue Mountains!"

"The wasteland is here, brother. *Here*!" Demba coughed a bubble of blood past his swollen lips. "You angered the gods when you refused to obey their natural laws—" He broke off as Kofi hit him again, then he continued, his voice weaker but still determined, "Chia must be called home. She is the rightful Chief."

"I am Chief!" *Whish!* The flywhisk sliced across Demba's face again, his brown skin stripping white, and then pinking into a deep red as the blood flowed from his wounds. "You will obey *me*!" *Whish!*

'Not the gods we cannot see and who desert us in our hour of need!" *Whish!*

Demba's head dropped forward and my other brothers let him fall to the ground. My mother, the thin silver bracelets she wore around her ankles shivering with her long keening cry, dropped to his side to wipe the blood away from his closed eyes to drip instead into the dry dust beneath his head.

Whish! Kofi hit him again, narrowly missing my mother's hand. "*I* am your Chief!" he snarled. "Remember that. Chia is dead by now and will never be Chief."

"I am not dead," I said. "I am here."

A silence greater than the silence that fell in the nights high in the mountains descended on the people gathered under the *khoro* tree. Dropping the small sack of my belongings to the ground, I stepped forward to kneel next to my mother at Demba's side. At the touch of my fingers to his neck, his eyelids flickered open. "Chiamaka!" As his eyes drifted shut again, his breath settled into a shallow, but steady, rhythm as he whispered, "My Chief!"

I knelt there, at his side, my head bowed low to hear him speak, my small woman's fist gripping the knobkerrie of the old *Makhadzi.* At his words, I felt a weight settle on my shoulders. As light as the breath of my noble ancestors and as heavy as the leopard pelt that proclaimed the position of Chief, it was the knowledge that I had waited too long to return from the mountains.

Slowly, to give my wobbly knees time to get used to the new weight they carried, I stood and faced my brother who wore the Chief's regalia. Stretching out the knobkerrie, I gently lifted the edge of the leopard pelt stretching across his fat belly. Now grown as tall as he, I was also lean and strong from my years of scavenging in the high, grey wastes that loomed over the valley.

"Where is my father?" I asked, and tapped that bulging belly of his with the knobkerrie. "Where is our Chief?"

With a howl, he grabbed the rain stick from me and snapped it across his knee.

"He is dead," he screamed. "Dead and buried these last ten years!"

"He cannot be dead," I whispered, shaken by the loss of my rain stick and the news I had already known deep in my heart. "He came to me last night and told me to return to the village."

A collective gasp flew up from the small crowd, and the wind swept it up, carrying it through the dying, dusty streets of the village until soon, even the oldest and the youngest of our people were clustering around the *khoro* tree, all of them murmuring and babbling.

"Chiamaka is here!"

"She is alive."

"Chiamaka, the Chief, has returned to save us."

Save them? How could I save them from the desolation that had greeted my return, when, without my rain stick, I could not even save myself? I could not make rain; I had never yet been able to make the Blue Mountains thunder and weep so that the ground grew thick with crops and the river ran strong with water.

"STOP!" roared Kofi. "*I* am your Chief!"

"You are no Chief," I said, "if your people are starving while you are fat and well-fed."

"You are an imposter!" he sneered, and threw the broken knobkerrie at my feet. "Where are the rains that you are supposed to bring?"

I remembered all the times I had not been able to make the rains come, no matter what the *Makhadzi* taught me. I looked at her broken stick, lying in the dust at my feet. And I doubted as he did, for I had never yet brought the rains to this land.

I looked at the faces before me. Gaunt, starving faces that stared at me with the same velvet brown eyes of the calf I had once saved in the cave of the glistening tears. In the distance, I heard the Blue Mountains give a faint rumble and a lone calf moaned its fear at the unfamiliar sound.

"The rains are coming," I promised and walked to where the sack of my belongings lay. "The lands will be watered and the people fed before the sun sets this day."

With only the sound of the calf lowing in my head and with an assurance I didn't feel, I withdrew what I needed from my sack. A porcupine quill to replace the rain stick; some *imphepo* to burn so that the sacred herb smoke could call to my father and to my father's father for help; and the cracked stone I had found the day I had dug the grave for the old *Makhadzi*.

Ignoring Kofi's shouts as he ordered the villagers to leave, to go back to their huts, I began to chant slowly as I packed the wild sage tightly into the fissure with the quill. To some watching, those too young to remember, it was curiosity that kept them in place; to others, the old ones, the ancient rituals I was preparing reminded them of an age gone by, when the world had been safer and food more plentiful.

My chanting got louder and louder as the mountains flashed and thundered in reply and the people and the village faded from my sight in the clouds of smoke. I flew high into the storm clouds and asked for the help of the gods; I begged their forgiveness: we, their people, had strayed from the path of the good spirits. In return for their mercy, I promised them a pure heart. Soon, the gods began to weep.

With a crack that shook wide the gates of heaven, just as I could faintly, oh-so-faintly, see my father and the old *Makhadzi* in the distance, a spear of lightning dropped me to the earth again where I lay with the smell of fire in my nostrils and my face pressed into the dust as it turned to rivulets of mud.

The sound of my people jeering and laughing forced me to push myself to my knees. Little blue flames still leapt along the blackened branches of the smouldering *khoro* tree, licking their way around Kofi's crumpled body, which jerked as the first stone was thrown.

"Imposter!" shouted an unknown voice.

"Thief!" cried another, and he mewled as more stones pelted his bare skin, stripped of the leopard skin that someone had thrown across my shoulders as I had lain exhausted from the rain-making.

"Enough," I said, for their relief was turning to anger and that in turn would anger the ancestors. Still on my knees in the dirt, I scrabbled closer to Kofi and removed my father's flywhisk from his loosened grasp. Before, when I'd touched it as a child, it had always felt too large for my hand, but today it felt light and easy in my grasp. Flicking it so it made a gentle *whish! whish!* through the air, I repeated my command, "Enough!"

One by one, the hands holding stones opened, the sharp, rough stones dropping to the earth as the people fell to their knees before their chief, who was I, Chiamaka.

After that day, Kofi was not the same: docile and obedient, he never uttered another word. He only sat, growing older as he stared at the world with the wide eyes of a child who had seen things he'd never thought to see.

Like the dry land, the ancient baobab tree took years to recover from the damage. But, when I was old and grey, and called my children to me the day I split my cattle amongst them, the tree, like the land, was rich and greenly abundant again.

A new trunk had grown, covering the scar of the burn with thick new growth. Not hiding it, no, for the past could never be hidden, but embracing it with new hope and new dreams so that both past and present formed one unified trunk that continued to shelter our people as we lived on in the shadows of the great Blue Mountains that had seen an eternity, and stood ready to face another.

An Ultimate Betrayal

I look at the letter, my heart thundering.

I want to unfold it and yet ... I know if I do, I'll have set in motion an irrevocable journey. One I'm not too sure I want to begin. I look at the clear black script; easily recognisable in its assertive characters and perfectly shaped loops. Why would she write to him at his office? What has she to say to him that she cannot say to me? That he hasn't told me of this letter taints something precious within.

My mouth is dry as I chew my bottom lip. The sharp pain makes the questions clearer and the answers less appealing. Annoyed with his carelessness, which made him leave the letter were I would inevitably find it, I push the letter back into the suit pocket.

Hours later, though, I'm drawn back to it. With shaking hands, I dig the heavy cream envelope from its rotten lair. Taking all my wavering courage in my hands, I slowly slide open the pages.

My serenity, my sense of who I am—flawed but loved, always loved—is forever changed. I drown in an instant, sinking into a sea of betrayal so deep I can never return to the shores of my previous life.

The life I lived before today, when he left his bitter, black secret for me to find, is over.

Escaping the Thunderbolt

"Isaac," Ma called over the baby's yell, "don't go outside without me!"

The brightly coloured grasshopper was far more alluring than Ma's usual refrain. It hopped onto the windowsill where he sat gazing at the mysterious clumps of lowveld beyond the rickety wire fence, which leaned haphazardly toward the winding dirt road that led to the farm.

"*Crrt! Crrt!*" he'd heard, and then it was there: the black armoured body with its bold bands of yellow, orange and blue; the square head with two long black-and-orange antennae twitching this way and that; and the six striped legs.

As it waited for him, he slid the window open, working the sash as quietly as he could so Ma wouldn't hear. The creature grew impatient and took off in a blur, settling just outside the gate on the gnarled old Nyala tree, its trunk split in two by lightning long before Isaac was born. Worried it would leave without him, he tossed a quick glance over his shoulder to check Ma was still with the baby, before dropping first one leg, then the other, over the sill to land with a quiet thump on the withered grass below.

"Hello, hopper," Isaac said, cautiously opening the gate so it wouldn't squeak and warn Ma. He walked to the Nyala tree with his hand outstretched but, before he could touch it, the insect stopped its vigorous crunching and, with a single thrust of its powerful hind legs, hopped up and flew clumsily from the tree to a bush, and then onto another. Chortling at this new game, Isaac followed it as it disappeared so deep into the bushes he couldn't see the roof of the house any more.

All he could see and feel were the haze of the sun and the dust motes in the air that rose as his shoes scuffed the sand, dry because the rains were late. He forgot Ma had said the bush was dangerous, for now his gaze was fixed firmly on the grasshopper. There was no danger in his mind; only the sound of his breathing and the sense of freedom until he was one with the still cacophony of the bush: the 'go-way, go-way' caw of the grey *loeries*, the rustle of the rising wind through the thickets and the fading "*Crrt!*" of his friend, the grasshopper.

"Stop," he panted, as it leapt ahead again and again, until he slowed to a stumbling walk because he could no longer see its rainbow legs or hear anything except the groan of the looming bushes and trees.

"Where are you?" he called, and tried hard to stop the tears gathering. He wiped a grimy hand over his cheek, and bent to pull up one of his socks. Ma was going to be mad when she saw how dirty he was, he thought, when—*if*, he gulped—he ever made it home.

Slowly, he twirled around in a circle. He was almost a man, he knew, but his heart stuttered wildly as he saw that the dust no longer danced in the sunbeams and the sky had turned the dull grey of the battleship Pa had taken him to visit when last they went to Simonstown harbour.

The rains were coming. He should be glad, but he was so scared that the murmur of adult voices came, for once, as a relief.

He listened carefully to where they came from and walked in their direction until he came to a clearing where three men, dressed in dark-grey suits, hunched around a pile of wooden crates. The bearded man, with his wide-brimmed cream fedora perched at a dangerous angle on the back of his head, was holding up a clear glass bottle, filled with a smooth amber liquid.

"The colour's right," he said. He brought the bottle to his mouth and—this impressed Isaac!—pulled the cork out with his teeth. He sniffed the open neck and nodded. "Smells right, too," he said.

The bearded man sounded nice, thought Isaac. So he left the cover of the bushes and, with a few eager strides, he reached the man. Tugging at his coat, Isaac asked, politely, as Ma had taught him, "Please can I have a drink, Mister? I'm thirsty."

He was about to add that he was lost too, but before he'd framed the words a thunderbolt cracked.

At first, as he lay in the dirt with his ears ringing and his cheek stinging, Isaac thought the storm had come as suddenly as the veldt rains did. But the two men on the other side of the pile of crates were scrambling to their feet, reaching for weapons Isaac hadn't seen earlier. Long ugly, grey things they were, but still neither man looked as menacing as the bearded man towering over Isaac, his fist raised and his pearl-grey spats planted firmly apart, as he lay there, helpless and afraid.

But before Isaac could cry out, he heard another sound.

"*Crrt! Crrt!*" his friend the grasshopper said, and landed on the bearded man's nose, the sharp little hooks on its legs holding tight even as the man screamed and slapped at his face as he stepped backwards, straight into the open crate. With a loud crash, the crate broke and the man fell, face-first into the other crates.

All Isaac could hear was breaking glass and shouting men and the urgent "*Crrt! Crrt!*" as his hopper flew past him into the bush.

He knew what to do. He scrambled up and, without even a glance in the direction of the flailing man, he ran as fast as he could into the bush the grasshopper had landed on.

When the noise in the clearing had died, one of the other men asked, "Should we find the kid?"

"*Ag* no!" said the bearded man. "He was too young. With the storm coming, he'll get lost. By the time they find him, he'll be dead or we'll be gone." His laugh made Isaac shiver. Only the soft *Crrt! Crrt!* at his ear slowed his heartbeat.

He turned towards the sound and saw his old friend. Gently, he lifted a finger a stroked the hammer-shaped head, smiling as the antennae tickled his skin. Looking into those beady orange eyes, he thought they were remarkably like Ma's eyes, when he'd done something he shouldn't and was in deep trouble.

So when the creature hopped from bush to bush, slowly this time, Isaac had no trouble keeping up with it. He followed it happily, trusting that, like Ma, it knew what was best for him.

Sure enough, just as the wind blew the last of the storm clouds away again, with one last bound and a loud *CRRT!*, the grasshopper burst out of a bush and landed, a startling splash of colour, on the bonnet of *Oom* Japie van Deventer's smart black police car.

Oom Japie was Ma's brother, and a *Sersant.* Isaac flung himself into his uncle's arms and told him about the bearded man and the bottles of golden liquid. He could even describe the clearing where he'd found them. *Oom* Japie swelled with excitement. "I know which clearing that is," he growled, and plonked Isaac in the front seat of his car. "Stay there!" he ordered, and called to his men.

It wasn't long and *Oom* Japie was back to drive Isaac home to where Ma stood under the wide-spread canopy of the old Nyala tree, the baby hitched on her hip, her eyes anxiously scanning the bushes beyond the old rusty fence.

Oom Japie forestalled her scold. “He’s a brave young man, your son,” he said, and ruffled Isaacs black curls. “He found the hideout of that gang of liquor thieves I’ve been after for months. There’s a reward, too,” he added, “£500.”

Isaac didn’t really know how much £500 was, but Ma’s gasp told him it was a lot of money. It was enough, at least, to buy the bicycle he’d wanted. And, although all the hot dry days of summer he often heard his friend the hopper calling and calling, Isaac never again went out into the bush alone.

The Gold Miner

From the time before the sun rose to melt the predawn chill, she waited.

She waited every year, on the first day of the Christmas month, because on that day her Father would arrive in the village, returning from his work in the deep, rich gold mines of Johannesburg.

Here, on the northern shores of the placid lake, she could not imagine what that far-away place was like.

"What is it like, Adada, down there in South Africa?" she asked every time he came home.

"The buildings block out the sun, for they are as tall as the mountains," he'd say.

She would rest her forehead contentedly against his thigh, looking up and up into his face, re-acquainting herself with its comforting plumpness and the hollows his smile dug next to his mouth. "Not as tall as you, Adada," she'd reply, and the furrows in his cheeks would deepen.

"The streets," he'd continue, "have more motor-cars than there are bees in a hive." Her eyes would widen at the impossibility of the thought; every Monday and Friday the old bus, its colours faded from age and the heat of the sun, trundled past on the highway near their village. She both loved and hated that bus, for it brought Adada home … but, in the New Year, it also took him away.

"The women," he'd say, "are not modest and hardworking like your Mama." He'd rub a hand over her head, softly rattling the yellow-and-white beads plaited into her dark hair. "A woman like you will be, Chiwa. Those women," he'd shake his head, his lips twisting with disapproval, "wear fancy dresses which shine like the moon on the lake, and their nails and lips are thick with blood-red paint."

"Are they pretty, Adada?"

"Not as pretty as you, my daughter," he'd answer as he swung her up in his arms. His hands calloused from his work and as wide as the footprint of the hippopotamus that broke the back of the boy from the next village, would hold her safe within their great strength.

Then would come the time she liked best.

He would lower his suitcase with a grunt of effort, for it would be heavy with gifts. The food would last them for months, until the money he sent from the goldmine arrived again, and they would leave the clothes and toys he'd brought in their packets, until everyone in the village had seen that they were new.

Last year there had been no gifts, for Adada had not come.

She had waited then too, plaiting and re-plaiting the reed basket she had made for him, seeing in her head how the day would go …

#

"Rest," Mama would say, gracefully hitching her pretty green *chitenje* up over her knees as she bent to take his shoes off. She would put them aside to clean, for Adada only wore his shoes again when he left. She'd pour him half a bowl of freshly brewed *mowa.* He would drink the beer in a few greedy gulps and then sigh with pleasure.

"No one makes beer like your Mama, Chiwa," he'd say. "Learn from her, and one day your husband will be as happy as I am."

She would laugh and run to fetch the plate of *nsima* she had cooked. She'd grind the corn herself and then boil it while Mama watched, teaching her how to scoop it from the pan before it was too dry.

When he was finished eating, he would strip off his shirt and run to join her brothers on the lake as they fished for the night's meal. But this night, before he went to the lake, she would take out her reed basket. "For you, Adada," she would say, "to put your fish in, so they don't slip away, back into the water."

"*You* made this, Chiwa?" Adada would ask, his hands stroking the rough edges as he turned the basket over and over ...

#

He had not come, and she had sold the basket to a yellow-haired tourist who had given her American dollars. She buried them under the giant sausage tree the village *sing'anga* used to cure the aching tooth.

After three full moons had passed, she heard that Adada *had* come home … only not to them.

"His woman lives in Catfish Bay," she heard Mama cry to the medicine woman, touching rough fingers to the lines beside her eyes. "She is young and beautiful, that's why he doesn't love me."

"The love sickness will pass," the *sing'anga* said and gave Mama a string of coloured beads to wear, and a bag of dried herbs to spread across the door. "They will call him back to you," the old woman said, "when the tourists arrive at the Bay Lodge and his other woman is kept busy."

Still he did not come, not even when the rains had passed and another Christmas went by.

Chiwa would not believe that Adada did not love them anymore. The last time she had seen him, when she had hugged his legs as hard as she could and cried that she did not want him to go back, for the belly of the gold mine would swallow him up so that he could not return, he had gently unhooked her hands and told her that he loved her. He loved them all, and nothing could keep him away.

When, once again, the first day of the Christmas month came and went, and Adada still did not come, and Mama cried and cried, Chiwa made a decision.

One Sunday night, when the night lights from the fishing boats lit the lake like stars in the sky, she silently slid from her sleeping mat, her bare feet making no sound on the hard-packed mud floor. With wary steps, she made her way to the old sausage tree and dug up her American dollars. She wrapped some fruit, some day-old *nsima* and her money in a piece of cloth and, balancing it carefully on her head, left the village to head in the direction of the highway.

Once, long ago, when they had sat together watching the dying embers of the cooking fire, and the distant rumble of trucks had drifted through the still of the night, Adada had told her how easy it was to find the bus stop. There, the bus that took him past the road to Catfish Bay, then on to Blantyre, and then all the way south to Johannesburg would arrive early in the morning.

"Then what, Adada?" she had asked.

"Then you climb up the stairs, tell the driver where you want to go and pay him."

"Is that *all*?"

Adada had laughed, his head thrown back and his teeth flashing white in the faint glow of the dying fire. "That's all," he'd said. "You have nothing to worry about—the journey is easy and safe; there is no danger. I will always come back to you."

When the noises of the night scared her and she skittered off the path, almost dropping her bundle, she reminded herself of his words. Eventually, she found the highway, just as the bus rumbled to a halt next to the crowd of people waiting at the side of the road.

"You're too young to travel alone." The driver, an old man with hair whiter than the clouds in the sky, said. "Where are your parents?"

"I am going to fetch Adada," she said and held out her dollar bill.

"If your Adada wanted you, he would come and fetch you himself."

She swallowed to free her voice from the sudden clutch of fears and tears. Pushing the crumpled note into his palm, she said, "He wants me," and climbed the stairs of the bus. The driver stood up but, before he could reach her, the big Mama behind him slapped her umbrella across the aisle.

"Leave her," she said. "She can sit with me," and shuffled up on her seat to make a small space. When Chiwa was settled, her feet resting on the bundle she'd placed beneath the seat to give her head a rest, the woman offered her a bottle. "Here," she said, "have some cola."

Finishing the drink, Chiwa murmured her thanks.

"Where is your Adada?" the fat woman asked, her eyes kind above the layers of chins.

"He was coming home from the gold mines," Chiwa explained, "but he got lost in Catfish Bay."

"When I was your age," the woman said, "my father worked in the mines."

She dug in the plastic bag she carried on her lap and took out a chocolate bar. Unwrapping it, she snapped it into two pieces. Giving Chiwa the smaller piece, she added, "He got lost on his way home too."

With the sweet taste of the chocolate on her tongue and the woman's comforting body next to hers, Chiwa felt strong again. "Did you find him?"

"I never looked for him," she said, and Chiwa was sure she saw moisture gather in her eyes. "But you will find your Adada," the woman said, "because you're a brave, clever girl. Now go to sleep. Rest your head on my lap, and sleep. Catfish Bay is hours away."

The sun was already low on the horizon when they arrived. Chiwa's breath came fast and shallow as she climbed down the stairs, her bundle on her head again and food from the big Mama in her hands. She watched the bus disappear until the woman's face was nothing but a brown blob in the distance and then she began to walk.

As the woman had instructed her, she walked down the road with the setting sun on her right, all the way past the red brick building with the grey corrugated iron roof and a big white sign at the door, marked with a red cross.

She carried on walking until the buildings became fewer and fewer and, at the fork in the road, she found the second sign.

Chiwa stopped a moment, peering through the darkening twilight to admire the hand-painted coffins and beds encircling the arrow pointing into the setting sun and the letters that, although she could not read them, the big Mama had told her said "Guayika Bed and Coffin Shop."

Finishing the bananas from the big Mama, she turned left, heading towards the sound of the lake lapping on the shore. This road would take her to the Bay Lodge, the place that kept Adada from coming home.

She shivered, more from the vastness of the night than from any real chill, and was glad when the dry, dusty road led her straight to the porch of the foreigner's lodge. Music thrummed through the air and she heard Adada's big, booming laugh above high-pitched squeals of women's laughter. But she decided to wait, for she did not want to speak to him in front of others.

What were a few hours more when she had waited so long already?

Although she had lived her whole life on the white-sanded shores of this same lake, here—many miles south of her village—the darkened waters looked forbidding. Yet she crept closer and, settling under a rough lean-to made of thatch and wood, took comfort from the silver trail of moonlight shimmering across the black surface.

She waited until, at last, the sounds from the buildings faded and the night sounds began to filter through the surrounding bushes. She waited even longer until, in the silence before the dawn sun rose to melt the chill away, she heard Adada laugh as he stumbled off the porch, finding his balance by grabbing the dead wood pole holding up her night's shelter.

Ignoring her aching bones and the stiffness in her knees, she leapt up and ran straight into his arms.

"Adada! Adada!" she cried, lifting her arms so that he could swing her to his shoulders and they could go home together. "*Muli Bwanji*?"

But, even as she asked how he was, her arms wilted like mopane worms burnt by the angry fire of the summer sun, for Adada brushed her away and, laughing, said to the woman who had followed him, "*Ai!* These street children can smell the gold on me. The government should do something about them."

All at once uncertain, Chiwa stepped back.

Had she made a terrible mistake? Was this some other man? Instead of a simple khaki trousers and white shirt, this man wore a strange red-and-black striped jacket, so bright it hurt her eyes. The yellow shirt hung loose over a plump belly, mid-way down trousers that flared over pointy white shoes. His eyes, too, were not Adada's gentle eyes, but the grooves beside his mouth were the same, as was the scar on the top of his shiny black head.

That scar, he used to tell her, was the sign of their ancestors protecting him. Once, deep, deep, in the white man's mine, a rock—glittering with gold—had fallen in the gully and, barely glancing a scratch on his head, had crushed the man standing next to him.

No, she thought, her mouth tightening with determination. This *was* Adada. And, because Mama said she was strong, like Adada, and just as stubborn, she reached out a hand and grabbed the end of that bright striped jacket.

"Adada," she said, tugging hard. For one sweet moment, she saw the old Adada flicker across the face of this strange Adada. She straightened, looking up into his face, but not as far up as she used to, for she had grown in the years since last she had seen him. "It is I. Chiwa, your daughter. I have come to fetch you home, for we miss you."

But he was still lost to her. With a hiss of annoyance, he pulled his jacket free and, turning to the woman, covered her red-painted nails with his large hands. He whispered in her ear and she guffawed loudly as the first rays of the rising sun broke free of the darkness, turning her dress into sparkles.

Chiwa trembled as the dying catfish trembles on the end of a fisherman's spear. And then, as the man who had been her Adada stopped and, leaving the woman, walked back towards her, her heart stuttered in hope.

"Adada …," she whispered.

"Here's a hundred," he said and shoved a red Kwacha note in her hand. "This should help your Mama." Then he made a shooing motion with his hands. "Go now. Get back to the village."

He stared down at her; then, swiping a broad palm over his sweating head, he strode back to the waiting woman.

Chiwa's mouth was dry, for all the moisture in her body was gathered in the corners of her eyes as she watched her Adada slide an arm around the young woman's waist.

"Goodbye, Adada," she whispered.

He did not look back.

She wondered if she would ever see him again.

She wondered how they would all survive.

And Chiwa wondered if she would ever wear a dress as shiny as the dress worn by the woman who stole her Adada.

The Gold Miner *first appeared in* Variations on a Theme*, an anthology published by The Literary Lab (USA) in March 2012.*

Read an excerpt from Judy Croome's DANCING IN THE SHADOWS OF LOVE**, a haunting spiritual novel in which three emotionally adrift women fight to heal their fractured worlds:**

Lulu

All I wanted, when the Prior arrived with new toys after the morning service, was to play with Taki and her friends. To be their friend.

Scrawny in his dingy chuba, the holy Prior looked like a crow proud of its scavenging. He pressed the tatty plastic bags, familiar with their red, blue and white logo, into Sub-Prioress Kapera's clasp and, as he always did, brushed close to whisper his secrets.

The toys were never new: a doll's clothes, mended with small neat stitches, and a painted truck, dulled by love. Other children had scuffed the newness off them.

That day the younger girls got a ball. We got a game called pick-up-sticks. The shabby box, held together by worn tape, had no instructions. Sub-Prioress Dalia showed us how to play. She let each of us have a turn, until we understood the rules.

When my turn came, I lay on my stomach, crouched close to the sticks because my eyesight already showed the weakness of my kind. I ignored the chatter of the other girls and, with steady patience, diminished the pile, stick by stick.

As the heap next to me grew larger while the one in front disappeared, the buzz of chatter sputtered out. Sub-Prioress Dalia murmured quiet words of encouragement until, as I picked up the last stick, she clapped. "Well done, Lulu! Look, girls, Lulu's got them *all*!"

Quivering at her praise, I held out the last thin spike. My grin must have looked foolish to the circle of faces around me.

"Ergh," said Taki. "The freak can smile."

"Don't look! Don't look! You'll go blind," another girl shouted. I never could remember afterwards who cried out. The howls of laughter bewildered Sub-Prioress Dalia.

"Stop!" she said. "Stop at once!" The meek threat had no effect and, above the chorus of taunts, she added a more forceful one. "I'll fetch Sub-Prioress Kapera to deal with you!"

The door slammed behind her, and they gathered around me like thunderclouds over an anthill. I hunched my shoulders and tucked my head between them as I began my appeal. "O Great Spirit King, warrior wild …," I chanted. Inadequate protection for what came next, I mumbled on as the first shoe struck, "Look upon a little child …"

It had always been clear that they hated me, except perhaps Sub-Prioress Dalia. "Pity my simplicity," I continued to whisper without hope that my plea would be heard. I did not flinch, because the kicks always came faster when they sensed my fear. "And suffer me to come to thee …"

Above the scuffles, we heard Sub-Prioress Dalia's steps, sharp with anxiety, as she returned. With one last kick, Taki said, "You'd better not tell on us, you child of the Levid, or it'll be worse for you." She cast a feral, warning glance at the others. "We'll tell the Controllers she tripped."

Today, I carry within me the rage born in that moment.

I snarled. A little snarl, one they didn't hear above their laughter as they gawked at me sprawled in front of them.

They heard the next one, though. It stunned them into immobility and I surged upwards, clenching the red pick-up-stick in my fist. The force I stabbed with pushed it backwards through my palm. I ignored the pain; even welcomed it, as the thin plastic toy became a nail lodged deep in Taki's leg. I will carry a small, round scar on my hand for the rest of my life. Nothing much. Not compared to my satisfaction at her yowl of pain, her pack around her as they bayed their sympathy.

Before they remembered me, I fled. This time, I didn't run towards the holding camp court, where the smell of incense and the nova high above the altar used to soothe me. For I had already begun to ask: when has the Spirit King ever answered any of my petitions? Instead, sucking the blood from my wounded palm, I ran outside. I ran through the rose garden I saw on my arrival—three straggly bushes of white roses the Prioress indulged herself with—and over the dry riverbed bordering the mountains until I could fling myself beneath the buffalo-thorn hedge. I crawled deep into the filmy branches, their gentle leaves and vicious double-hooked thorns my protection. For aeons, they have collected the spirits of the lonely dead returning home from exile. There, in their dark silence, I was always welcome.

Jamila

The full moon shone over them and turned the world silvery surreal. Jamila drank in the sight even as she drank from her wine glass. The mellow air, the silence of the night, trickled into her blood with the alcohol. When Samanya bent his head and touched his lips to her neck, she sighed and raised a hand to stroke his cheek to see if it was silky golden as it looked.

Samanya turned her into his embrace. He kissed her lips, her breasts, her secret place the night air cooled even as his lips set it aflame. Soon, Jamila shuddered out a release as Samanya moved between her legs and showed her paradise.

"Why?" she sobbed later. She leaned back into the low balcony wall and held her pale pink sweater, another gift from Dawud, against her nudity. She never wore pink again, not after that night. "Why couldn't you leave me alone?"

Samanya riffled through her bag and took a tissue. He wiped himself clean. "You were too innocent, Jamjar," he jeered. He laughed a sunless laugh that almost, but not quite, drowned out the rasp of his zipper jerked back into place and dropped the soiled tissue into her lap. "Much too innocent."

Where once there was a warm flicker of hope in all that the city offered her, the extent of its insidious underbelly chilled her. "You're horrible! Horrible!"

She longed for Dawud to save her from the nightmare. He was not there and, unprompted by any thought, her hand searched for her pendant, her Spirit King-mask, to give her strength, to cover her shame revealed by the brilliant, merciless gaze of moon and man. But she had stopped wearing it when Dawud had bought her the real gold necklace she'd asked for.

Samanya laughed and coolly tucked in his shirt that, in the heat of ecstasy, she'd torn lose from his trousers. He said, as he left her, "Whatever I am, Jamjar, you're the same." He looked at her with remorseless calm and added, "Because you could've said no anytime."

And there—right there, where the moon's light rippled across the dark waters of the silent sea—Jamila accepted that she had found her passion and kissed the face of her ezomo.

Zahra

My time is close.

My hair is grey and I smell of the wintergreen ointment I rub on my varicose veins when they ache, which, these days, is most of the time. My breasts, those silken sacs that my husband had so loved to fondle, have long since succumbed to the cancer. When I undress, I stare at their flat, scarred remains on my chest. They got what they deserved, those pieces of flesh. Once the weapons of temptation that were Little Flower's ezomo, now they are where they belong: ashes in a hospital's hellish incinerator.

I have been lonely. Lonelier than I could've imagined since I lost my husband Barry. He died twenty-five years ago but, except for the memories he left behind, he was gone from me long before then.

And my son. My little Barry. Grace used to call him an angel and he never lost that smile in his eyes. It only gleamed with a different brightness when he brought a young woman home, nineteen to his twenty, and laden with his child in her belly.

"You're too young to marry," I said.

"We're in love, Ma. We want to marry."

I often think he must have been smiling, when they died, the two of them, in a distant land as they fought to save the lives of those wounded in a war that should never have begun and has yet to end.

"People aren't collateral damage, Ma," he said the day they left for South America, his face wrinkled with the same determination he used to climb up and down stairs that were bigger by far than he. "We want to help. It'll be an adventure."

"Foolish boy," I snapped and buried my tears in the warm baby smell of my grandson Dawud. "Kiss your son goodbye."

His answer was a laugh, as reckless as always, and I never saw either of them again. But I had my grandson, as placid and malleable as his grandfather Barry.

Until Dawud, too, decided he wanted to go to war.

Read an excerpt from Judy Croome's a LAMP at MIDDAY**, a lyrical volume of poetry that both laments and celebrates the mysteries of life, love and grief:**

Where the World Ends

There, where the blue sea meets the indigo sky,
Is where the world ends.

I stand alone, in my red coat and yellow boots,
Faded and shabby with use.
I clasp a thick, gnarled staff,
Made of oak or elm, I know not and care less.

The sea breeze brushes my cheeks with damp fingers,
Smoothing away the silver tracks of loneliness,
Even as the orange-and-green striped sail
Of a passing catamaran
Billows with the fierce joy of movement
Age and illness have so long denied me.

Dancing over the playful white caps,
The cat bears away,
Into the distant horizon that beckons.
I lean forward, far over the cliff edge,
Watching until it falls into nothingness.
I throw away my staff and wonder:
Will I ever be as free again?

And there, where the blue sea meets the indigo sky,
I stare into infinity and watch the world end.

(First published in ITCH-e09 September 2011)

Hero Worship

How hard it is to remember what was
When I a small child and you a grown-up hero:
Daily reality has me grasping at straws
Of old images I stoop and pick up.

The cheering of a scattered crowd
Rising to their feet at the hard-hitting sound:
You struck the ball right to the moon
With bases loaded and two runs to win.

There you were, on the next day, boldly splashed
Across the front page of the Bulawayo Chronicle:
High above the ground, flying into home base,
White uniform unsoiled and a pompadour of debonair dark hair.

Somewhere in the years gone past
I've lost both you and that crackling paper icon:
All I have left is a sad doppelgänger,
A grey-haired child who reminds me of you.

(First published in a Lamp at Midday, *Aztar Press, 2012)*

Haiku

morning tea

your cup steams. you blink
and yawn until your jaw cracks
the sleep from your eyes.

giraffes

long necks undulate.
gentle eyes and jigsaw coats
crown a setting sun.

peeling an onion

wholeness diminished
stripping layer by layer
to find my centre.

(First published in a Lamp at Midday*, Aztar Press, 2012)*

About the Author

Judy Croome lives in Johannesburg, the economic powerhouse of Africa, but her childhood playground was the Zimbabwean bush. With the beat of Africa in her blood, her writing is set in this continent, which has deep passion as its heart.

The driving motivation of her writing is the search for love in all its forms. Judy writes because she believes words have great power: they can bring comfort, joy and hope. They can reveal secrets and lies. And, while they may not change the world, they can—at their best—change people's lives, even if only for a moment.

Judy is married to Beric Croome. A vegetarian, Judy loves her extended family and all cats, and she enjoys reading, writing, nature, old churches with their ancient graveyards, evolutionary astrology, meditation and silence.

Other Works

Other works by Judy Croome include the compelling spiritual novel *Dancing in the Shadows of Love* and a volume of poetry *a Lamp at Midday* (Aztar Press).

Short stories from this collection have been included in the print anthologies *Notes from Underground* Anthology and *Variations on a Theme* Anthology (The Literary Lab) and *The Fall*: *Tales from the Apocalypse* (Elephant's Press Bookshelf) and on-line magazines *The Huffington Post Featured Fifty Fiction* and *Itch-e Magazine*.

Coming Soon

Coming soon from Judy Croome: *Watch for the Morning*, a full-length novel, will be published by Aztar Press in 2014.

Connect Online

Join Judy Croome on her social media network. You can find Judy here:

Web: www.judycroome.com
Twitter: @judy_croome
Pinterest: Judy Croome (jcroome)
Goodreads: Judy Croome
Facebook: Judy Croome
LinkedIn: Judy Croome
LibraryThing: Judy Croome

Please Help

If you have enjoyed these stories, please consider leaving an online review on Amazon, Goodreads, Loot, Kalahari, your personal blog or any other book review site of your choice.

Printed in Great Britain
by Amazon.co.uk, Ltd.,
Marston Gate.